Indecent
EXPOSURE

Jonathan Thomas Stratman

For Billie

The life that I have is all that I have
And the life that I have is yours
The love that I have of the life that I have
Is yours and yours and yours.
—Leo Marks

iii

CHAPTER 1

We went out from town by dogsled, at minus thirty-five degrees, to collect the earthly remains of the gambler, Frankie Slick. He'd been found the previous day, face up in a snowdrift, along the river about five miles below town. It was a painfully bright day, with sunshine reflected intensely off a million facets of icy diamonds set into the surface of the drifted snow, but there was no warmth.

The five-dog team, happy to be on the trail, barked and yelped with their warm breaths visible in the frigid air. To quench their thirst, they snatched mouthsful of airy fresh snow as they ran. We made good time on a perfectly flat trail, over six feet or more of solid river ice.

A scrap of red flannel knotted to a willow branch called us back to the frozen rise of riverbank beyond which Frankie lay. The flag was a sensible precaution against further snowfall and the chance of not finding him again until spring—or never.

There were three of us, the two Athabascan moose hunters who found him, and me. Mission-schooled, the Indians preferred not to touch him until he'd been blessed. As the priest of the group, that was my job.

"The Lord be with you," I said, my breath an icy cloud.

"And with thy spirit," murmured the two ex-altar boys.

Dropping my moosehide mitts to hang by their braided cords, I fumbled the pages of the Book of Common Prayer in my woolen work gloves. It had been a long season of burials and I now knew the words by heart, but found that as a newly ordained priest, holding the book still gave me confidence.

"Unto God's gracious mercy and protection we commit you. The Lord bless you and keep you. The Lord make his face to shine upon you, and be gracious unto you. The Lord lift up his countenance upon you, and give you peace, both now and forevermore. Amen."

"Amen," echoed the mushers.

It wasn't in the prayer book, but I found myself saying what my predecessors in this place had said: "Oh ye ice and snow, bless ye the Lord."

"Amen," said the mushers again. They were in no hurry and would probably like it if I'd just keep praying for a while. Blessing or no, they weren't in any hurry to have to deal with the body. It wasn't that they were particularly squeamish, it was that Frankie had managed to die—and freeze solid—completely spread-eagled, arms and legs thrown wide against a wind-riffled mound of blown snow. It wasn't going to be easy to get him back to town.

On a Sunday afternoon in late November, my sermon delivered, I would usually be sitting in a squeaky wooden office chair at the tiny newspaper office, sipping a scalding cup of really bad coffee and reading a baseball game off the Associated Press teletype.

Of all the things I could miss about life in the States, like fresh oranges or cow's milk in glass bottles, the only thing I did miss was live baseball on the radio. Especially right now. For the third time in four years, the perennial champion Yankees faced their long-time rivals from across town, my team, the Brooklyn Dodgers. Of the Dodgers' seven World Series setbacks, the last five had come at the hands of the Yankees. I thought the Dodgers had a real chance at the pennant this year. Too bad I was three thousand miles away, staring at a frozen dead man.

I raised my eyes from Frankie's peculiar frosty squint to the brilliant blue bowl of cloudless sky. This place I stood—thigh deep in drifted snow—lay one hundred miles south of the Arctic Circle, some four thousand miles from the seminary I'd left in Tennessee, and a million miles from life as I'd known it. I wondered again how I'd gotten here. I could work on that later. The question of the moment was, how did Frankie get here and how would we get him home?

Though ours was a very small town and I knew almost everybody, this was the most time I'd spent with Frankie. I found myself staring, not so much at his face as at his expression. The expression seemed more familiar than his features.

"Okay to move him, Father?" asked one of the mushers, my first friend in town, Andy Silas. I nodded. Andy and his cousin, Jerry Charlie, had been tracking a moose along the river ice, then up over the bank and here to this little willow thicket. They'd had two pieces of bad luck. First the moose gave them the slip and then they'd stumbled, almost literally, on Frankie.

Frankie was missing for at least a month before anybody noticed. There hadn't been much of a search because, with absolutely no clues, there didn't seem to be a place to start. Besides, he was a professional

3

gambler, moneylender, and small-time thug, known for making life difficult for others. Finding him like this was no surprise.

The real surprise was that they'd found him at all. It was pure dumb luck to stumble on him here, and especially to find him before the wolves did. Although finding him after the wolves would have made it easier to get him on the sled.

Andy and Jerry each grabbed one of the rigid wrists and prepared to lever the body out of the drift. "Wait," I said. That expression on his face was one I'd seen in France during the war when I served as a medic. I remembered it from one particular German soldier I'd examined—a suicide.

Wading deeper into the drift, I brushed the frost off Frankie's prominent chin and lower jaw, pushing the wolverine parka ruff tight against his neck for a better view. I found what I was looking for: a small bloodless bullet hole beneath Frankie's set chin. I saw no hole, nor sign of blood on the back of his parka hood, so figured a relatively small caliber bullet had entered there, bounced around inside his skull and snuffed him.

"Look here," I said. "Frankie killed himself."

"Cheez!" Jerry shuddered, taking a step back. 'Cheez,' I'd learned, is what a Mission boy learns to say instead of something like Jesus or Jeez, expressions likely to earn him a thimble whack on the top of his head if the deaconess hears him.

Andy whistled. "Suicide?" He shook his head. "Nah. That don't sound like Frankie." But he dropped to his knees, brushing back the snow beneath Frankie's outstretched right hand, searching for a gun. He nodded at his cousin. "Check his other hand."

"Nothin'," said Jerry.

Rocking back on one knee, Andy regarded me over the top of his dark glasses. "No suicide," he said. "Unless Frankie shot himself back in town, then walked out here to fall down. Don't make sense." He looked around at the distant tree line and the clear expanse of frozen river, then back at me. "Ask me, Frankie finally pushed somebody too far and they shot him. I can't even think of someone who deserved it more than he did."

Color seemed to bleed from the day, and suddenly, irrationally, I felt the hair stand up on the back of my neck. I admit the notion of being out here with a murdered man scared me. Something like murder wasn't supposed to happen where I was and I resisted the urge to look over my shoulder, as though the shooter might still be loitering in the drifts.

I turned to look at them. "You're right," I said. "It's likely he was murdered." Neither Andy nor Jerry changed expression. As I looked at them and they looked at me, the distance between us seemed suddenly very wide. I was out here along a frozen river with two men I didn't know all that well, who said they'd found him. They'd be most likely to find him here if they left him here. Maybe I was part of the alibi. Maybe I was just paranoid.

"So let's get him out of here," I said. They nodded and each grabbed a wrist, hauling the corpse spread-eagled across the snow toward the dogsled, as I followed.

I'd only been in town for about five months, and already had heard Frankie's name linked to gambling irregularities with dogsled races, area ice pools, prostitution, loan sharking, and extortion. Down at the

5

Coffee Cup Café, when his name came up, I'd always listened to see if anybody would say, 'Aw, Frankie's okay, you just gotta get to know him.' Nobody ever did.

So either he wasn't okay, or nobody ever got to know him, or they did get to know him and liked him so little they shot him, pointblank, and left him to feed the wolves.

Not to be judgmental, but I've always wondered what a lowlife scum says when he meets God. I think I know what God says: "I've been waiting for you."

CHAPTER 2

Word about Frankie spread quickly. Of course hauling him back to town by dogsled, raised and spread like a sail, may have had something to do with it. The sleeping bag we'd brought to bundle him in was useless. We finally jammed one frozen hand down between the sled slats, and balanced him on that hand and the corresponding frozen foot, so the other hand and foot angled skyward. We tied him between the sled rails and draped him with a tarp, sewing the grommets closed with moose hide lacing. It worked, but just barely. With Frankie on the sled, and only five dogs pulling, I expected to be walking back. But no, Andy and Jerry wedged me into the back corner of the sled, half standing, steadying the corpse.

"Can we sneak into town?" asked Jerry.

"We don't have a prayer," said Andy, then he looked at me. "Do we?" They grinned and finished securing the dead man.

Just on the edge of town we had to stop and adjust the tarp, which had slipped, revealing a bare, slightly blue hand that had lost its heavy mitt and seemed to be waving to spectators.

It began to look like everyone had heard the news. As we made our way up the street, a dozen or so people came out of the post office, the general store, the Coffee Cup, and the town's two saloons, to walk along

7

by the sled, and banter. "Now that's a stiff," someone said, and everybody had a laugh.

A man is dead, I thought. But bringing in the body of Frankie Slick seemed more like a holiday. Andy must have guessed my thoughts. He shrugged.

"Frankie was born here," he said, "lived here and died here. But he never was *of* here. And if there's anybody in this whole place that Frankie didn't screw— sorry Father—I don't know who it is." He gestured at the impromptu gathering on the street. "When you live like that," he said, "you die like this." He looked directly at me. "Save your sympathy for his victims."

Stashing a corpse midwinter in Alaska is never a problem. They keep indefinitely, or at least until breakup. Sometimes we put them in the parish hall, a World War II surplus Quonset hut. The arched-roof metal building is unheated storage for surplus clothing and medical supplies that churches in the south forty-eight send out for distribution to the needy. Which is nearly everybody in town but the late Frankie.

Imagining a surprise encounter between frosty, splayed Frankie and some of the church ladies, we opted to stow him in Andy's meat locker, an empty eight-by-ten bear-proof cache. It should have been filled with hanging moose meat, but wasn't, due to an extra-cold winter and a severe shortage of anything to shoot.

We speculated again about how we'd get him into a coffin. True to form, Jerry suggested borrowing a meat saw from the general store. But we left Frankie intact, lying in the middle of the floor, ringed with baited mousetraps, and I went to call the marshal.

It was four o'clock by the time I got back to the mission office, an extra room in the log cabin I call

8

home. Already full dark, the temperature had fallen to minus thirty-nine and an entire universe of stars shone brightly from an obsidian sky.

I made the call, dialing the five-digit Fairbanks number from memory. Since I arrived in early July, I'd called the marshal approximately twice a month for deaths by drowning, fire, gunshot, and all the complications of alcohol. The worst call was late summer, when one of my parishioners drank too much and went to sleep on the railroad tracks, only to be split nearly in half by the Southbound 10:10.

"This is Father Hardy—Chandelar," I said when the assistant picked up, and then answered his usual terse questions. "Yep, again. Bullet." There was never any small talk from the assistant. "Right," I said, which was my way of assuring him that no one would have access to the body before the marshal got here.

As a seminarian, I had imagined "tending souls in God's garden," whatever all that meant. In reality, the U.S. Army had better prepared me than St. Luke's Seminary. The tiny town of Chandelar, on the Tanana River, was a hundred miles from Fairbanks, and eighty miles or so from Mt. McKinley. Nenana, the nearest 'big' town, had a population of maybe five hundred, compared to our three hundred on a good day. I didn't see how we could keep that number up, given the rate of deaths, and I found myself wondering if anybody around here ever died of natural causes.

I heard my outer door open and close, preceding a firm but gentle knock on my office door. "Come," I called, and she did.

In a town like Chandelar, you know everybody by about day three. The people you are aware of on days one and two are either the people you think you

9

want to know, or the people you think you probably don't want to know or people you'll have difficulty knowing. This was one.

Her name was Evangeline Williams, known as Evie. She lived alone with no obvious means of support and was generally thought to be a business partner, in some delicately avoided way, with the late Frankie Slick. Jesus knew prostitutes but this was the first one I'd met. I admit I didn't know what to expect.

Standing just inside my study door, pulling off mitts and unzipping a heavy caribou parka, she rotated slowly as if memorizing titles on the shelves that lined the walls.

She was at least half Indian, taller than most at about five foot seven. Her hair was nearly black and pulled back in a ponytail, which she shook from her parka hood. She had dark eyes and high, Athabascan cheekbones. Evie wasn't beautiful, but had something that made men want to look at her. I mean, more than just availability. Her half smile suggested she knew something that was funny and it gave her a kind of glow.

"You heard about Frankie?" I said, rising. The glow dimmed.

"Yes. But that's not why I'm here."

Her voice surprised me. Not Athabascan, not from low in her throat, spoken with a tight jaw. Her voice was higher, almost musical, and she had a bright, clear way of shaping sounds, as though she'd been practicing.

"Okay."

"I understand that you can help me make a will."

"Are you in danger?" I asked. "Does this have something to do with what happened …?"

"Forget Frankie," she said, and smiled a little, like she was being patient with me. "Can you do a will?"

"It's called a holographic will, and you do it. It has to be entirely in your handwriting, and I can help you. But …"

We were facing each other across my desk, and without warning she caught my wrist and drew me around to her side. Smoothly, quickly, with her free hand, she unbuttoned her plaid flannel shirt, pulled it open, and raised the man's white cotton undershirt she wore, exposing her breasts.

My breath caught. I was stunned. I looked to either window, then the door, to see if we could somehow be observed. The glow started again, and a low, musical laugh.

"You're blushing, and speechless! How long has it been since you've seen a woman's breasts?"

I didn't answer but must have winced. "Your wife," she said. "I heard. I'm so sorry … that was cruel."

I finally found my tongue. "No, it's a year now, and I …" And I didn't really know what to say. Mary's sudden death from polio, during the last epidemic, still left me speechless.

I sometimes get strange looks if I mention that my wife has died. A lot of people still think only the Roman Catholic Church has priests, forgetting Russian and Greek Orthodox, Church of England Anglicans and their American counterpart, Episcopalians, whose priests all marry and have families and somehow still

11

manage to serve God while administering to their fellow man.

Mary and I planned all this together. Being missionaries in Alaska, doing good for people who really needed it. Building a family and a life in the wilderness. She died in Tennessee, just months before my graduation, ordination and journey north. Now she was gone and I was here alone in my office with a bare-breasted prostitute.

She sat and drew my hand to cup her left breast. Her lower breast was cool against my fingers, but the top of the breast, under my thumb at about eleven o'clock, was raised and hot.

Our eyes met. "You need to go to Fairbanks on the morning train. You need treatment, maybe surgery."

"No," she said, releasing my hand. "I actually only need two things, and I need them from you. May I have them?"

"Well yes, of course."

"I need you to help me with a will."

"Okay, and … what else?"

"I need you to not tell anybody about this. I need you to be silent. You're a priest, right? That's one of the things you do."

"Yes," I said. "It is. I will. But …"

She pulled down her undershirt, buttoned her shirt and, businesslike, drew a list from her pocket. I sat facing her, handed her a pen and paper and dug for a brochure I'd sent for, even though by now I knew it too, by heart. In addition to funerals here, I did a brisk business in wills.

Late that night, in bed but unable to sleep, I admit I thought again of her breasts. They seemed like beautiful breasts, and the first I'd seen in a long, lonely time. It was grossly unfair that one of them was killing her.

Which snapped me back abruptly to the killing of Frankie Slick, Evangeline Williams' former partner. Today I'd met my first prostitute. Now it occurred to me to wonder if I'd also met my first murderer.

CHAPTER 3

Just after six a.m. the town generator conked out. It was only a half block away, housed in a ramshackle garage, so the roar of sudden silence woke me. I snapped the switch on the bedside lamp and was still groggy enough to be startled that the light didn't come on.

Extending an arm into the thirty-five degree room, I lit a candle—better than cursing the darkness—grabbed the red leatherette *Book of Common Prayer* I keep at my bedside, and burrowed thankfully back down under my mound of old woolen army blankets and goose down.

I read, "The Lord is in his holy temple: let all the earth keep silence before him." In the absence of the generator, the silence was palpable, and blessed. It seemed right for praying, though I'd be happy enough to hear the generator come back on when they got it refueled, or relubed, or whatever it was.

Although I had a small woodstove, my tiny congregation insisted I had better ways to spend my time than cutting firewood. So they'd sent to Fairbanks for a used oil floor furnace and rafted it down from Nenana. It had taken several of us two days to get it installed beneath the cabin floor and running properly. So now I had instant heat—as long as I had electricity. All I had to do was click the thermostat and then I could dress standing on the grate with hot air blowing. Some mornings in a bathrobe, I felt like a recent movie photo I'd seen of the young actress and sexpot, Marilyn Monroe.

Back at St. Luke's, Mary and I got out of bed for our morning prayers. It had become the right-feeling way to begin the day. Here, I hadn't gotten out of bed for morning prayers since mid-October, and probably wouldn't until after breakup in the spring. It was just too darn cold.

"Oh Lord," I read, "save thy people." Then I began to replay the previous day's events. I saw Evangeline William's face and tried to figure out what I could do to save her. I had promised to keep her secret. And there was certainly no way I could force her to Fairbanks for treatment, even assuming they could treat a thing like that there. They'd probably want to send her to the States, to Seattle. If she were unwilling to go to Fairbanks for treatment, going to Seattle wasn't likely. I admit I thought about getting someone to fly in to treat her here—highly unlikely also—but realized that I'd have to tell them what was the matter to get them to fly in, which was what she'd asked me to not do.

"There's no way on earth I can help her," I said to the empty, cold room. Which is when I realized what I could do. At that point the generator fired up and my bedside light came on. The moment seemed filled with meaning. "Amen," I said. Blowing out the candle, I jumped out of bed and went to dress on the furnace grate. I had a plan. Even if I had absolutely no idea how to make my plan work, it felt better than having no plan.

15

The telephone rang at eight thirty. Since few of my congregation had phones, it rang infrequently. The two or three rings it took me to thread my way into the still-dark office allowed time to become a bit nervous about who might be on the line and how it was going to complicate my life.

"Episcopal church," I said. "Father Hardy."

"Father." It was Frank Jacobs, calling from his office in Fairbanks.

"Yes, Frank."

"Fogged in here, Father. Ice fog. Weather service says it's likely to last all day."

"Right," I said.

"So just hold on to the stiff, okay Father?"

"Certainly." I don't know what else he thought I would do with it.

"And uh, just make sure nobody messes with the body, okay?"

"It's locked up," I said.

"Great. That's just great. See you tomorrow about noon." As I hung up, I found myself thinking what an odd business his was. He spent a considerable amount of his time managing the dead. Examining, transporting, collecting, disposing. Even though I'd already had more than my share of fatalities, I still felt lucky that most of my job consisted of helping to improve the lives of the living.

My first 'customer' arrived at about nine, and I opened my door to the soft glow of predawn gathering behind the hills.

"Mr. Moses," I said. He startled a bit, like he wasn't used to being recognized. It seemed an odd reaction since he was the town's closest thing to a celebrity.

16

"Father, can we talk?" I waved him in.

This was my second non-parishioner in as many days. Funny how things seem to come in waves. During the past year, Teddy Moses had come from out of nowhere to become one of Alaska's top dogsled racers. If he did well in the upcoming season, there was talk of traveling to race in New Hampshire. For a musher from Chandelar, that would be like racing on the moon.

I noticed his parka, commercially made and down filled. Unusual in a subsistence town where actual cash was scarce and most people had to make things themselves or barter. His mukluks too, were some kind of canvas with a reinforced sole.

A superb athlete, it was said that one reason he won was that he rarely rode. Most mushers would run a bit, then ride the runners for a bit. Not Teddy Moses. By all accounts, he was the most obsessed, driven-to-excel person in the entire Territory of Alaska. So far, it was making him a winner, probably the next North American Champion, but I wondered fleetingly what kind of price he paid for being like that. There was always a price.

Absolutely confident in his abilities, he would tell anyone that he was the best. In fact, Andy Silas and I overheard him in the Coffee Cup one morning—the whole place did—saying just that.

"Is he that good?" I asked as we left the restaurant.

"I seen him," said Andy, "run twenty miles behind a dogsled at thirty below, and not show the wear." I could believe it. Moses walked and moved like spring steel. The Fairbanks newspaper, the *Daily News Miner*, had already nicknamed him the reigning "Iron Man" of dogsled racing.

Now seated, Moses and I stared at each other. Flipping back his parka hood, he smoothed the Brylcreemed blue-black bristles of his stylish, flattop haircut with the palm of one hand. Uncharacteristically tongue-tied, his lips moved, but no sound started.

"Just begin at the beginning," I said. I don't know why I thought he had come to see me, but his first words, and the way they grated from his throat, gave me a chill.

"Frankie Slick," he said. And then the 'Iron Man' began to weep.

It turns out, Frankie Slick's other talents included loan-sharking. When Teddy Moses needed cash to push into the dog-racing 'Big Time,' he made the mistake of going to Frankie to get it. It wasn't long before Slick had him dancing like the organ grinder's monkey. The first loan, not very big, didn't cost very much. The third loan, for $10,000, might not have been that much, stateside. But here in cash-poor Chandelar, it was probably four or five years of Moses' total earnings, and it cost him everything. He had signed over his cabin and property, half of everything else he owned, and half of anything he might ever win. But that still wasn't enough.

"When I couldn't make the payment," he sobbed, "and I went to him …" The musher lost control of himself completely and slid off the chair onto his knees. "He told me to forget the loan, he'd cancel it."

I wasn't following. "Cancel it? In return for what? You didn't have anything left to take, did you?"

"My daughter," he wailed. "Slick wanted to trade my daughter for what I owed him. That was all he wanted. Everything! He promised he wouldn't hurt her." The musher went down in an incoherent pile on his hands and knees on the floor, slobbering, weeping and moaning.

"He wanted her for … what?" I asked, fearing the answer.

"Photos," sniveled the musher, "just photos. No touching, no sex, he claimed, just photos."

"And what did you tell him?" I asked, though the answer seemed clear.

"I told him yes—I had to. I didn't mean it—just to buy myself some time to figure out what to do. I mean, it was just pictures, for Chrissake! It'd be like she was helping to earn her own way a bit, you know what I mean? Do you know how *hard* it is to carry this whole thing on my back? Dogs, sleds—d'ya know how much it costs to feed fifty dogs every day? And …"

I held up a hand. "I know this isn't the Christian thing to say," I said, "but shut up! The snake showed up with an apple and you gave him—rented him your daughter. You don't even deserve to have a daughter."

He buried his face in his hands and made the kind of sound a living heart would make if you pulled it out beating and slowly ripped it in two. I'm always amazed at people who think that hell comes later when it's clearly right here, right now, and frequently of our own making.

"So you bought yourself a couple of hours and did what?"

"Well, I went back to tell him the deal was off and he could take everything and be damned. I thought I'd saved the day, but he'd already found Roberta, and told her. She knew it was true, knew I'd be ruined and so she said yes to the bastard. So in the time it took me to get back to him, I'd already lost everything." At that, the musher jumped to his feet. In a single motion, he went from down on his hands and knees to standing fully erect with one hand jammed deep in his parka pocket. I got to his wrist before the muzzle reached the side of his head, but the pistol fired, the room filled with smoke, and I thought my eardrums would burst. Moses folded up in the chair weeping and I was able to wrench away the gun, a short-barreled thirty-eight. I dropped it in my desk drawer and turned the key. The bullet hole in my ceiling would leak come spring.

I knew the girl. Everybody knew the girl. Roberta seemed a spot of sunshine in a gloomy season. She was slight and pretty, with a thick braid of shiny black hair reaching almost to her waist.

"Alright," I said when he finally wound down. "Tell me the rest."

He turned his face to the floor and mumbled. He'd sent his wife to Tanacross, to visit her family when the girl began her 'job' for Frankie. All she had to do was turn up one day a week at Slick's cabin, ready to pose. Slick was in no hurry. He'd treated her well, even taking her to Fairbanks for one of the days, buying her just about anything she fancied. On one of her sessions, they actually talked about the deal he'd made. Slick told her she could go home and forget it, and he would simply take everything her father had. The family would break up, but he'd make sure she was okay. Again, she wouldn't hear of it, and kept the bargain, showing up as required and, apparently, taking off her clothing to pose.

She hadn't had anything to do with her father since, except to drop a payment receipt in his lap each time she returned. Now her mother was home and had found out from others. There was a price all right: steep.

Finally he ran out of sad tale and sat up, red-eyed and puffy-faced. "Slick was the devil," he said.

"Slick didn't sell his daughter."

He considered. "You're right," he said. "I did."

"So what are you going to do about it?"

"I don't know what to do about it. Everything I've done so far has been wrong. Everything is gone. Now I don't even care about the fucking championship." He grew instantly contrite. "Sorry, Father. My wife is packing to leave; she's already got a ride to the train. My daughter won't go with her, but she won't have anything to do with me, either."

"Slick's dead," I told him. "He's got no more hold over her." Then the suspicion. "Did you kill him?"

"No," he said, startled. "I didn't kill him. I was racing in Anchorage until yesterday. I came home with a thousand dollar first prize. I figured it was my last chance to try to buy my family back from Slick. And then he was dead, but I didn't kill him."

"Can you prove it?"

"Sure."

"But the marshal's on his way. If the weather clears, he'll be here tomorrow. If he finds evidence of your business deal—like nude pictures of your under-age daughter—you'll go to jail anyway. And maybe you should. Your job was to protect your daughter, not trade her for an easy ride."

"Oh God! I know. Can you help me?"

I started to tell him I had no idea how to help him, but then abruptly I did have an idea. "Maybe," I told him. "But if I can help you, will you help me?"

Moses sat up a little straighter, with a guarded look in his eye. He'd made one too many bad deals recently and I could only imagine what he might be thinking.

"I've got to check some things," I said, "but here's what you do. Are you with me?" He nodded cautiously. "Go to the church—it's open—and pray. Tell the Lord what an ass you've been, and how you're willing to do anything you can to make it right. Then go home and say the same things to your wife and your daughter. Got it?" He nodded.

"And how am I going to be helping you?" he asked.

"We'll get to that later," I assured him. "But it's nothing you have to be ashamed of." I looked at him hard. "You're a champion. You've always told anybody who'd listen that you're tough and you have what it takes to go the distance, no matter how difficult. Didn't you say that? I heard you say that."

"Yeah, I did."

"Now prove it."

Then he looked at me and shook his head. "I never heard you say nothing, but I think you're pretty tough yourself." He stood up and zipped himself into his fancy parka, nearly smiled, and went out. I watched him through the window as he made his way along the canyon of shoveled trail to the church, went inside and closed the door.

I didn't feel tough.

CHAPTER 4

It was nearly eleven o'clock before the sun ambled up. Not that it mattered. A dense layer of ice fog and wood smoke swirled around my cabin, obscuring even the church, just thirty-some feet away. I tried to busy myself with paper shuffling, pencil sharpening and letter writing but I couldn't forget that lack of visibility made this the hands-down best time to take a look at Frankie's place.

With my thumb, I melted the ice on the inside of the living room window behind a mission-barrel curtain someone had felt compelled to install. It was nearly gaudy with a meant-to-be-whimsical tropical motif that included palm trees, beach balls, frothy breakers, and bathing-suited frolicking couples. Peering past all this beach gaiety, through the thumb-sized hole in the ice, I could just glimpse my thermometer: minus forty-two degrees. The insides of the door hinges were white with frost, as well as walls behind curtains or furniture. Another cold day in Chandelar.

The news about the Moses girl made me feel sick, and for the first time since coming here, I found myself thinking that maybe I was in over my head. Maybe the job was just too big for me. Then I found myself laughing. Of course it's too big for me, that's why I pray.

But I didn't think prayer alone was going to get me into Frankie's place before the marshal arrived. It was the only way I could see to keep Teddy Moses, his daughter Roberta, possibly Evangeline Williams, and God knew who else out of trouble over this.

Since I now knew that Frankie's day-to-day livelihood had been loan-sharking, I also knew he'd have kept a concise record of his business dealings. Sins of the entire village would be on display there, every mistake, every bad decision, every late-night moment of weakness. So, to right all these wrongs, the priest was actively seeking a way to commit a burglary. It's certainly not what they'd taught me in seminary.

What would Mary say about planning to break in and steal evidence so that people who had clearly sinned could avoid being punished? She'd say, "Who made you judge and jury? Who made you God?" Would she say that or was I saying it to myself? Or, knowing Mary, she might be right by my side handing me the flashlight. It was times like these I missed her the most.

On the other hand, I didn't think God wanted Teddy Moses in jail, the family split up, and Roberta carted off to one of the Indian schools. At least that's what I told myself as I pulled on my parka and headed off up the snow-packed street, through a swirl of icy fog.

A few moments' brisk walk and I was shaking a massive padlock and rattling the hasp, thankful for the thick layer of fog but feeling exposed nonetheless. Frankie's was the only cabin in town, and probably the only cabin in the entire Tanana Valley, including Fairbanks, with tiny barred slits for windows, up high on the walls like a fort. So it was no particular surprise to find the door locked. It was probably the only locked door in the whole valley.

I tramped around the cabin, through snow that had drifted thigh high in places, interested to note that someone had already tramped here before me. The cabin was one-story with a corrugated metal roof, set back a bit from the street with no immediate neighbors. An unadorned rectangle, it had been constructed of logs too long and thick to have come from anywhere in this valley of small birches and cottonwoods. The tops and bottoms of each log had been carved flat so they fit together perfectly with no gaps to chink and tar.

Out front stood Frankie's brand new, light gray, 1955 Ford pickup truck. An extension cord ran out to the engine oil heater from an electrical outlet near the cabin's solid-plank front door. Cars and trucks without such heaters wouldn't be starting until after breakup in the spring. When Frankie plugged that in, he thought he'd be driving it soon. Now he was stretched out frozen solid on the floor of a meat-shed and he'd never be driving it.

I stared at the truck for a long moment, with what I admit was a nearly unforgivable case of pickup truck envy. "Not for me," I said to the wind, "for the church." And I continued on my way around. But there were no other doors and I would probably have to be stripped and greased to get through the windows, even without bars, which wasn't going to happen.

I rattled the hasp again with the same result, then slunk away into the fog, praying to make it back to the rectory before anybody got a good look at who was thinking of breaking, entering, and carrying off evidence in a murder case.

~

I perked a pot of coffee to have with my lunch. Then I sawed off thin slices of lean, nearly frozen

25

moose meat from a dwindling roast I kept on a shelf in the small vestibule behind my kitchen. I'd been out hunting several times with Andy, Jerry and others, but we'd yet to bring down—or even see a bull moose. It could be a long, meatless winter.

Once or twice a week, I'd whip up a batch of sourdough pancakes for breakfast, eating the leftovers like sandwich bread the rest of the week. Mary had been the cook. I couldn't seem to make even simple things work. My specialties included way too many pancakes, mush—burnt on the bottom—scorched popcorn, and crunchy rice. I was probably ten to fifteen pounds lighter than last June when I got off the train in Nenana. I guessed my 'failure to thrive' was starting to be noticed.

Three weeks ago one of the older ladies in my congregation, Violet Jimmie, had reached out and pinched my cheek after early service, which puzzled me. The next morning her grandson arrived bearing the first in a series of casseroles—this one, home-canned salmon and noodles—with orders to start eating.

Although I worked on my sandwich earnestly, it didn't really taste like anything. Nothing had since Mary died, and I left about half of it. It wouldn't go to waste. There were about thirty sled dogs chained in front of doghouses on the adjoining lot. They were happy to help me out with leftovers, even blackened oatmeal.

There were times, like right now, that Mary seemed close enough to talk to. In fact, sometimes I even tried talking to her, but wasn't comfortable with the way my voice sounded in the empty room. There were plenty of Alaska stories of old-timers with cabin fever who talked to themselves—and answered. I hadn't been here long enough, or drunk enough cheap whiskey or fortified wine to be talking to myself. There was still time. Even so, I said, "I miss you." And then, I sat silent, listening for something. Anything.

Out in the yard at nearly forty below, a low whistle of wind sighed around a drifted corner, raising nothing more than a little rattle of beaded snow. It wasn't the sound I'd been hoping for. It was like nothing so much as the tender murmur of someone you loved deeply, moving away.

~

The afternoon passed in a comfortable, timeless blur of ordinary. Molly Joseph, nearly full term, arrived at the door in search of baby clothes. She seemed to examine me, a little like a pithed frog, as I pulled on mukluks, parka and mitts for the journey across the arctic street to the still-fog-hidden Quonset hut. There under the dim, bare, hanging light bulbs, the warm, moist vapor of our breaths occasionally mingled in the minus-thirty-degree room, which briefly made us seem like comfortable friends enjoying a chore together.

Breathing the scent of old clothing, we dug companionably through cardboard boxes and scattered piles, finally coming up with enough to get an infant launched.

"Our birth is but a sleep and a forgetting." Wordsworth said it. *Forgetting what?* I wondered. Rooms with God in them? Other better lives? In the instant of death would we happily pick up that old thread again? I didn't know. But I liked the idea that as Mary gasped away from me she strolled, all pink and warm, up to a green place where friends waited. How I envied them.

When I come out here and dig through all these old clothes, I often have thoughts of death and Mary. I think it's because most of these clothes are from people who have died. Their relatives swoop in, scoop up all the stuff they want and shove everything else into boxes to ship off to Alaska missions. Sometimes their reckless hurry worked in my favor. In the last shipment, I found enough cash in abandoned trouser pockets to send out for a case each of diapers and Vaseline.

And because of the churches that particularly supported this mission, I knew that these trousers, shirts, suits, and natty sport jackets had come from people who died in Boston, Cincinnati, or Chattanooga. For many of them, their clothing traveled farther than they did in their lives, except maybe the vets who had been to Europe with me, or to the Pacific.

From the chicken-wire lockup, for safekeeping new things purchased with contributed cash, I pulled one of the fresh diaper bundles, a new blue baby blanket embroidered with a yellow duck, and a wonderful fresh jar of Vaseline. I'd reached the point where new stuff made me feel almost giddy.

"Blue for a boy?" I offered. Molly giggled a little and ducked her head shyly beneath her wolverine ruff. It was nice to know I hadn't lost my ability to talk to women.

Then, maybe a bit regretfully, for my part, we were finished, and Molly waddled off into the fog with her big parka belly and bundle of baby treasures as I went back to my empty rooms.

I finished the last of my current casserole, moose burger with potato and noodle, and settled with a cup of sweet tea to read the nearly current issue of the *Saturday Evening Post*. The magazine came by steamship from Seattle to Seward, then by rail to Nenana, and out to Chandelar in big canvas bags by pickup truck.

So the September issue arrived mid-October and I was just now finding the time to sit down with it in late November. I'd been savoring one article in particular, on Al Kaline of the Detroit Tigers. He'd been signed right off the Baltimore sandlots only two years before, and sent to the Tigers without playing a single game in the minors. In his second season, he hit his second career homer—a grand slam—making him the second youngest ever to do so.

So it was just me, the tea, Al Kaline and the ticking of an old Regulator clock, until the phone rang. I could feel my pulse jag up as I threaded my way into the darkened office, fumbling for the desk lamp at the same time as I picked up the receiver. "Hardy," I said.

"It's Andy."

"Andy? Where you calling from? Is something wrong?"

"Teacher's place," he said. "Look, I think you better come down to my place. Somebody's broke into my meat shed and messed with the body. Can you come?"

"Sure, I'm on my way." I hung up the phone but stood for a moment, just beyond the pool of lamp light, pondering the concentric rings of trouble that started with Frankie Slick, alive or dead, and spread through the village.

The ice fog had gone, leaving the sky perfectly black and impossibly deep with stars. To the east a whip-crack curtain of blue-green northern lights furled and tumbled and hissed. One dog howled nearby, then more in the distance, then silence. There was no moon, but starlight reflected off snow made the way clear and there were no sounds but a soft crunch under my mukluks and the random cracking of frozen trees.

I met Andy and Jerry at the meat shed. Their faces were grave. Andy's flashlight revealed the open door and crowbarred hasp, the padlock hanging useless. We stood considering the damage.

"The body?" I asked.

"It's there," said Andy. "Uh …"

"What?"

"You'll see." He gestured toward the door with the beam of light.

The first thing I saw was that the mousetraps had been removed. As a result, much of Frankie's face was gone, his nose and lips—probably his eyes. I'd seen worse in France but this was bad enough. "Ugh," I said, looking away. "Marshal isn't going to like this." Pushing back Frankie's parka ruff, I checked under his icy chin for the telltale bullet hole, just to make sure it was really him.

Andy squatted next to the corpse. "Here," he said. He grabbed one of Frankie's pants pockets, which had been turned inside out and cast a shadow like a rabbit ear in the flashlight beam. "Not gonna like this much, either."

All Frankie's pockets had been turned out; even his pants had been undone and opened. The casual debris of his life: pocket change, matchbooks, crumpled Tareyton cigarette pack, a couple of twenty-two caliber live rounds, a pocket knife, a comb—three silver dollars—all lay where they'd been dumped.

"Oh boy," I said. I felt like a prize dunce. I used to do this in the Army, processing the wounded or dead, including turning out their pockets and bagging their effects. Here, we'd simply put Frankie on ice and left that chore for the marshal. Big mistake.

"Why didn't we search him?" I said. "Dumb." The way Jerry turned to look at Andy told me something. "Did you search him?" I asked Andy.

Andy looked back at Jerry with an expression I couldn't read, but didn't have much trouble imagining. "Yep," he said.

"Wallet?"

"No."

"Gun?"

"No gun."

"Letter of any kind?"

"Nope."

"What then?"

"Key." He looked at me directly, too directly I thought. "Looks like Frankie's house key." He held it out to me. "Here, I think you better have it for safekeeping."

CHAPTER 5

"How are we going to lock this place?" I asked.

"Plywood," said Andy, and produced most of a nearly new sheet from around the side of the shed. That much new three-quarter-inch plywood was like gold in Chandelar.

"Where did you …?" I started to ask. The large, white, stenciled letters read, 'Property of U.S. Government.' "You didn't … steal it, did you?"

Andy shook his head. "The dump at Clear. Sometimes they throw out whole sheets of this stuff. Like new. That's the Government for you. My cousin brought five of these sheets home by dog sled. Took him most of two days. Plywood was like a big sail. Every time he got sideways with the wind the sled blew over. Said if he had a pickup truck he could have filled it and gotten home a lot quicker. Imagine what you could do with a whole pickup truck full of new plywood." The three of us stood silent for a moment, lost in the wonder of it.

"Do you know who did this?" I asked them. Jerry looked away. Andy looked directly into my eyes but neither answered. "I'm not asking you to tell me who, but I mean, do you know who?"

"Plenty would like to," said Andy.

"What I'm asking is …"

"I know what you're asking," said Andy, almost sharply. He took a breath. "No, I don't know who did this. I do know that I could have sold tickets for it. Hold this light," he said, and flipped off his mitts to dig in his parka pocket for nails. "Somebody tries to pry this off, I'll hear 'em." He turned to Jerry. "Gimme that hammer."

"We need to put the traps back," I said. "You probably have some more, don't you?"

Neither Andy nor Jerry moved for a long moment. Again I felt like an outsider, like a white man from the States.

"Yeah," Andy said finally, "you're right. Jerry, I think there's a cloth sack of them just inside the back porch there." Jerry loped off down the path.

"He was evil, Father. Evil as fucking Hitler or Mussolini. You don't have any idea how …" I raised my hand.

"I've been getting the idea," I told him. We stood silent and I could hear the snow crunching under Jerry's feet as he came back. "You believe in God, don't you?"

"You know I do."

"So tell me," I said, "where is Frankie now?"

"In the shed with his face ate off?"

"Nah. That's just his body. Where is the rest of him?"

"I don't know. You mean like … hell?"

"Worse. I think Frankie is having to explain himself to God."

Andy considered the notion. "Shit," he said finally.

We replaced the traps and nailed the plywood over the door. Then we said goodnight and I headed home. The road was smooth and easy to walk, though high shouldered with about four feet of plow-thrown snow and the occasional buried car. On the road surface, a foot or more of snow had been packed solid, then glazed with a hard layer of sun-melt, though not slick with the temperatures so low. Even ice isn't slippery at twenty or thirty below.

About halfway home, I stopped and flipped back my parka hood, exposing the back of my neck to shockingly cold air. Turning my face up to the star-filled bowl of deep black sky, I felt small and dismal and as dry and lonely as a box of cold rocks. As if in consolation, a meteorite traced a long, slow, golden arc across the full field of my vision, and I felt better. I finished my walk home.

I was nearly asleep when the fire siren went off, and before I even knew I was awake, I found myself standing erect in my bare feet on the freezing linoleum floor. I never hear a siren without thinking I'm back in London and it's an air raid. Worse, after the last Chandelar fire, I'd buried three children. Who would have thought, in a place so cold and often dark, that something bright and hot could be so cruel?

Adrenaline fueled, I was dressed and out the door while still zipping up my parka and pulling on my mitts. There wasn't much to be done about a fire with the temperature this low. There were only a couple of hydrants in the whole town, and they were useless, valved off over the winter to keep them from freezing to pieces. The town kept the fire hall heated, so there'd be one tanker of water to fight a fire, assuming the tanker would even start. It was war surplus, but I'm not sure which war.

I had no trouble following the smell of smoke, the echoing crackle, and the exquisite waves of shimmering heat. As I drew nearer I could make out the pungent smell of raw gasoline. It was all leading me in a familiar direction, to the log home of the late Frankie Slick. Someone had poured a stream of gasoline low on one side of the cabin and lit it. I wondered if anybody would turn out to fight this, or if we'd all just stand around it like a football bonfire and somebody would lead cheers. Maybe they'd bring weenies.

I heard a shout. "The tanker won't start."

"That's it then," I thought, relieved, and a weight lifted. I could feel Frankie's key against my leg in my right pants pocket. I was off the hook. I had been absolved. I felt nearly giddy watching the flames beginning to climb the log wall, knowing there was nobody inside to try to rescue, nobody to bury in small caskets when the ground thawed. Around me, I sensed a general air of people relaxed and at ease. I heard greetings called out and distant laughter.

But then I heard another more ominous sound, the roar of the power company's grader, also kept in a heated garage. It came bounding and sliding on huge rubber tires, up the snow-slicked road, full speed, the bucket lowering as it reached Frankie's yard, to slide a massive mountain of snow right up against the base of the burning cabin. Backing up fast, and then driving ahead twice more, it was abruptly all over but the sizzling. And everything seemed very dark again.

"So I'm not off the hook," I said.

Andy appeared from a cloud of smoke and steam. When I looked at him he threw up his arms.

35

"Hey, I didn't do it." For some reason it was funny and we stood laughing together. "Sorry about before," he said.

"It's okay." We stood companionably silent, watching people arrive late, realize the show was over, mill around a bit and then head for home. Andy had quickly become my first friend in Chandelar, my only friend, really. We had the war in common. I was a corpsman in France and he was a sharpshooter in Italy. He told me once that he had come home to Chandelar because out in the States, where whites lived, he kept seeing the faces he'd seen through his scope. Although he could go for months without, sometimes whiskey was the only way to dim those faces. So many ghosts.

I didn't tell Andy what I was planning—I wanted to—but I knew he would want to come along. No, not just want to come along, expect to come, because he always seemed ready for anything. But I knew it was wrong to allow him to get involved. Not that breaking and entering, possibly stealing, seemed that right for me.

So I said goodnight to Andy and once again walked the frozen streets home. I went inside, turned the lights on, and in a few minutes turned them off, as though I'd gone to bed. *In case anybody's watching*, I found myself thinking. Who would be watching? And why? I hadn't even broken in yet and already I felt guilty. "It's a logical by-product of seminary and the ordination," I told myself.

The key turned easily in Frankie's lock and the door swung silently inward. I closed it soundlessly, and shielding the flashlight with my hand, ventured a look around. I needn't have worried. Inside the tiny, fort-like

36

windows, were heavy fort-like shutters, all closed and bolted. With a sigh, I snapped on the overhead lights.

The room formed a large rectangle, with a small bathroom and closet interrupting the back cabin wall. Next to the closet, several feet of cardboard boxes were stacked nearly eight feet tall, each with a neatly typed list of its contents. An old Remington typewriter perched on its own metal stand nearby.

A small kitchen was arranged on the right wall, complete with an apartment-sized Westinghouse electric range and even a small Frigidaire. As though we didn't have enough frigid air just out in the yard.

Frankie may have been a creep but he wasn't messy. His coffee mugs were un-chipped, washed and hanging from a wooden rack. His refrigerator was neat and orderly, and unlike the last one I'd owned, nothing in it had sunk into itself and begun to reek.

I had always thought that houses were like churches in the sense that everybody has an altar. For some people it's the radio or television. For Frankie, it was a massive Wilkes & Bodie frontier safe, mounted on heavy, spoked, steel wheels about six inches in diameter. Wheels or not, it wasn't going anywhere. Frankie had also gone to the trouble of chaining the safe to a pair of heavy iron loops, built into the massive log structure of the wall.

"Where's the combination, Frankie?" I asked, but nobody answered, which was probably a good thing under the circumstances. A faint haze of wood smoke hung in the air—from the evening's arson I realized—and my eyes stung. There was another smell, out of place, a little like the way mayonnaise smells. Photo fixer! I remembered it from college. Which reminded me that, among other things, I was looking for photos.

Bookcases stood on either side of the safe, each about three feet wide and six or seven feet tall. Most of the books were brand new, with bright leather bindings. I pulled one from the shelf. It was H.G. Wells' *The War of the Worlds*, which surprised me. Frankie didn't seem like the classic literature type.

On the opposite wall, a gun rack held no less than a hundred rifles. Dowels, drilled into the log walls, displayed maybe fifty handguns. It took a moment to realize what I was seeing: a pawnshop! It was filled with possessions of the people of the town. Possessions he'd cheated them out of. No wonder they hated him.

I tried the handle on the safe, just in case. No luck. Even trying it was laughable. Everything in the room that was worth anything was chained in place. All the rifles, all the handguns, everything.

I turned a slow circle in the room. If I were a combination, where would I hide? Someplace unlikely. I tried the freezer in the Frigidaire. Again, no luck. Something kept drawing me back to the bookshelves. If it were my combination, I'd hide it in a book. Not that it meant Frankie would. But which book?

One of the few books that showed use was a photography manual, but he hadn't written in his combination. Same with his Monkey Wards catalog. A two-year-old copy of *Playboy*, with Marilyn Monroe on the cover, probably looked most thumbed. I hadn't seen one of those since seminary.

Everything else—all those fancy leather-bound books—looked nearly brand new. Of course you didn't have to read a book to hide a combination in it. But he hadn't written the combination in *Moby Dick*, or *The Man in the Iron Mask*, or any of the others I thumbed through. *Why would a guy like Frankie own a collection of books like this?* I wondered. I resisted the urge to take one home and read it myself.

Think! I thought. Where would he be most likely to hide the combination? Which title? On the top shelf, a copy of Hudson Stuck's *Ten Thousand Miles With a Dog Sled* caught my eye. An Alaska book. That seemed likely. But it wasn't. It was as lightly used as the rest. Stuck, also an Episcopal priest, was one of my heroes. I had practically devoured his books while I was in seminary.

So then I thought, if it's not in the most likely book, which is the least likely? And that's when I saw the Bible.

At the far right of that shelf was an old, faded, seemingly much read King James. If I thought it held wisdom or guidance for Frankie I was wrong. It had been painstakingly hollowed out to cradle a pair of small, silver Derringer handguns, like gamblers used to wear up their sleeves, although one was missing. There was more. Penciled inside were three numbers that looked very much like a safe combination. So it had offered guidance.

The safe's old-fashioned tumblers nearly made a racket in the silent room. Left, right, left, and—*click!* I wrenched the heavy handle around and the huge door sighed itself open. Inside, the center of the safe was honeycombed with compartments, each holding at least one old-style accountant's ledger.

It was all there, written in Frankie's light, neat, distinctive hand. So much loaned, so much taken, the payments, the incredible unpayable interest. The real mystery about Frankie's death was why one of his customers hadn't shot him sooner.

One book, fatter and more worn, kept careful track of Frankie's shadier deals. I started reading at the back and quickly found Teddy Moses' name and the record of his daughter's payments. This book was the one I was looking for. The rest, however disagreeable, was just business. This was the one that would hurt. I stuffed it up under my parka, into my belt.

Stacked at the bottom of the compartment, I found the photo boxes. There were six of them, each about an inch thick and stuffed with prints that Frankie had developed himself. I found the pictures of young Roberta Moses in the top box. Every other box held more. Different faces, the same shame. A pillowcase from Frankie's bed, still imprinted with the stain of his greasy head, would carry the lot.

I went to close the safe but thought better of it. The marshal would come tomorrow and the inside of the safe was one of the things he would expect to see. The quicker he did see it, the quicker this whole thing would be just a memory. At least that's what I told myself.

Turning off the lights, I eased myself out the door, relocking the padlock. Outside, nothing had changed. I heard an owl hoot softly in the distance and somewhere a wolf howled. He sounded lonely, too.

I sneaked home. There's just no other way to say it. Sneaking wasn't a thing I liked or was used to. I kept looking back over my shoulder to see who might be following, to see who might be watching the priest break into the home of a dead man and carry off his belongings like a thief in the night. Very like a thief.

I made a brief stop in the church, without turning on any lights, and paused a moment in front of the altar to connect. *Am I doing the right thing?* What would Jesus do? Would he let everybody take the fall for his or her various sins and omissions? Because they deserved it? "What Jesus would do?" was always my litmus test. Would he protect the innocent, like young Roberta? I thought so. I hoped so.

And then I was safely back in my cabin. It was four a.m. and I had found what I'd gone looking for. But I was too tired to feel successful, too tired to feel much of anything, except alone.

Maybe if I went outside and howled.

CHAPTER 6

The murmur of the distant Cessna turned to a roar as the ski plane buzzed us at fifty feet, made a tight turn into the wind and swept down for a graceful landing on the snow-drifted river ice. The nearly midday sun, low in a brilliant blue-white wash of sky, reflected blindingly off the silver wings and struts. Even wearing sunglasses, I squinted.

Andy and I stood in a brittle wind beneath a flapping orange windsock. We waited as the Cessna taxied up to the tie-downs, the engine cut and the prop stopped. I felt terrible and hoped it didn't show. My late-night crime spree—and four a.m. bedtime—had left my stomach in knots. For once I'd actually been asleep when Andy came knocking at about eight, and the usually enjoyable morning visit with coffee and small talk felt forced and awkward.

"You okay?" he finally asked.

"Oh yeah," I said, "rough night." Which was true. I'd slept fitfully, with dreams of being dramatically unmasked by the marshal in front of Mary and a gathering of my parishioners. It was a dream that then degenerated into being unexpectedly naked in public and unable to remember my high school locker combination and find my first class.

Steady, I told myself. *An hour or two and he'll be gone and everything will be back to normal, except that someone here—almost certainly someone I know and talk to—is a murderer.*

I've never been comfortable with not telling the truth. Even trying to get something like a birthday gift for Mary, telling some little story to mask the truth that I'd been shopping never worked. She always knew. I would blush and stammer and the harder I tried to come up with something reasonable, the more ridiculous I sounded.

Now I'd gone from trying to fool my wife about a birthday trinket, to trying to fool a U.S. marshal about facts relating to a murder. While my motives might be pure, at least in my mind, last night—while not sleeping—I had been unable to even count the number of laws I was probably breaking. Now, here I waited on the riverbank to greet and talk to the last guy I should be anywhere near. It occurred to me that maybe I should just confess right away and save him the time and trouble of exposing and humiliating me.

As the plane taxied up, I was surprised again that the marshal had come alone. Although I shouldn't have been; he was known for it. It was said he couldn't abide the notion of having the Territory of Alaska pay a pilot to fly him out and then do nothing but wait. So on his own time, he learned to fly.

Marshal Jacobs opened the door and handed out his satchel which Andy grabbed, and then stepped out on the strut and down. We waited while he unfolded a padded robe, like a mover's blanket with leather straps, and tossed it over the cowling, buckling the buckles underneath. At this temperature, it would help keep the oil fluid enough to restart, but only for about an hour.

He was slight, wiry, about five foot eight, dressed in official olive drab and leather. He had steely blue eyes behind military-issue amber-framed spectacles and a precise regulation mustache. He wore a service forty-five in a flapped holster on his hip. Instead of a hood he wore a brimless hat with long earflaps that met and fastened under his chin, leaving the back of his neck exposed. I'd have been frozen dressed like that but the marshal didn't seem to notice.

Walking up, he pointedly looked around us as though we might have happened to bring Frankie's body along to save time. "Victim?" he said. His dislike of government waste extended to communication and he always spoke as though he, personally, was being charged by the word.

"My place," said Andy. "Four blocks," and he pointed.

"No truck yet, Father?" he said, also looking as though we might be holding out on him. The last time he came down on business, we had to borrow a pickup from Henderson at the General Store, to get the coffin over to the railroad at Nenana. It's true, I could think of fifty ways to make use of a truck, but getting one to make the Federal marshal's job more efficient was definitely not one of them.

So the three of us started walking—marching really—at a vigorous clip down the road toward Andy's.

"Give me the facts," he said.

So we told him—me somewhat breathlessly—as he stepped along smartly. I resisted the urge to trot. But he stopped abruptly when we got to the part about the missing face.

"Thought you locked it."

"Did," said Andy. "Crowbar." Now Andy was doing it.

The marshal looked at me. "Still sure it's him?"

"Bullet hole," I said, pointing under my chin. Now I was doing it. Andy couldn't quite suppress a grin and had to look away.

"Took the traps, huh?" The marshal shook his head. "They must have hated him." He pulled out a leather pocket ledger and made a note.

Jerry, who had been instructed to start pulling nails when he heard the plane, was pulling the last couple as we double-timed into the yard. He looked from one of us to the next with half an idiot grin on his face but wisely said nothing.

The marshal examined the crowbarred padlock hasp, photographed it with a camera from his satchel, and made another note. He jerked a leather-gloved thumb in the direction of the corpse. "Lived in town?" he asked. Andy nodded. Which reminded me of something.

"Key," I said. I have Frankie's house key. Pulling off my wool glove, I dug for it in my pocket, and handed it to him.

"House key? Somebody searched him but missed the key?" he said, his eyebrows up.

"I searched him first," said Andy. There was a long pause while the marshal seemed to be measuring him, probably for a cell. "Yeah," said Andy. "I found the key and kept it out—in case you wanted to see the house before you saw the body." The marshal looked at him for another long moment, then made another note.

"Good idea," he said.

It occurred to me to wonder why Andy kept the key instead of putting it back in Frankie's pocket. I'd been so wrapped up in questioning my own motives it hadn't occurred to me question his.

"So if you searched the corpse first," said the marshal, "you can tell me, is anything missing?"

Andy shook his head. "Nothing. All thrown on the floor," he said. "You'll see."

Marshal Jacobs turned to me. "Thanks," he said, which I took to mean he was through with me.

I turned to go, feeling relief beyond measure. "Around later?" he asked.

"Sure," I said, but he had already stepped into the meat shed.

"Ugh," I heard him say.

I sat for about fifteen minutes, staring at the telephone with the butterflies in my stomach doing wingovers. Finally I dialed the number and he answered on the first ring, sounding tight, tired—defeated.

"This is Father Hardy," I said. "We need to talk."

"Talk?" he said. And then I could hear the smallest bit of hope start up in his voice, maybe the hope of hope. "Did you ...?" he asked.

I interrupted him. "Can you stop by the rectory?"

"Now a good time?" he said.

"Good as any." I heard the click as he hung up, then the dial tone. I went over my plan—again—for the twelve minutes it took him to walk from his house to mine. When I answered his knock, Teddy Moses wasn't alone.

"My wife," he said. "Effie." I stood aside and they came through the door together and went straight into my office. On the surface of it, they didn't look like a set. He was tall for an Athabascan and she couldn't have been even five feet. He was still wearing his store-bought parka and mukluks, while she wore a simple cloth parka and moose-hide mukluks she'd likely sewed herself.

Although they looked like they were going to their executions, they were holding hands, which seemed a good sign. Mary would have approved, which made me feel a little better about my plan, and worse because of the recurring realization that she wasn't here and wouldn't be. I wondered how many years I'd have that daily jolt. Of course she would have disapproved of every other aspect of my plan, a notion that brought my butterflies winging back. *Oh well.*

I went in behind them and closed the door.

"How did you …?" he asked.

"Let's just say you're off the hook."

In unison, they began to breathe again. Color flowed back into their faces and I saw him squeeze her hand.

"Thank you," he said.

"What you did was wrong. It was terrible."

They hung their heads together. He said, "I know."

Effie gave me a tight look, head still slightly down, eyes intense. Her first flush of relief had been tainted by the suspicion of something left owing. "If you feel that way, why are you helping him? Why not let him be thrown into jail and punished—as he should be? Why let him off?" Tears welled in her eyes and tracked down her cheeks, but she held her gaze, her face set.

I took a breath. I felt out on thin ice. I've never believed in the classic version of hell. I've always thought that the place most people call hell is inside us. If I'm wrong, if there is a hell, I think I just confirmed my reservation.

"I don't think God wants you punished," I said. "I think God wants you to get it right. And I'm not letting you off. I explained to your husband that there is a price to pay. But I'd like to speak to him about that alone. Please?"

She looked at me hard and I thought she'd refuse, but in the end she climbed out of her chair, went out the door quietly and closed it gently.

Teddy Moses sat up straighter. Now he was expecting the blow. I couldn't help but wonder what kind of terrible thing he thought I might do to him. "Do you believe in God?" I asked him.

"Not your God," he said. "Not the Episcopal God."

"That's fine," I said. "But just for the record, because it's my job, I think there is only one God. Not an Episcopal God, or Methodist or Catholic or Buddhist. I think all that is as trivial to God as the shirts we wear. But here's how it works, at least how I've been taught that it works. You need to confess your sin to God, and then as God's agent I will absolve you in His name and assign your penance. A penance is what you have to do to make up for your sin. It's a kind of trade. You're not really off the hook until you complete your penance. Okay? Get it?"

"Yeah," he said tentatively.

"Okay. Kneel."

He looked at me like I'd asked him for a sexual favor. "Here?"

"Yep."

Slowly he slid to his knees.

"Now you say this: Forgive me Father for I have sinned."

He said it.

"Name your sin."

"I sold my daughter." He put his face in his hands and began to weep. I gave him a minute to pull himself together and then I absolved him of his sin in the name of God. When I told him what his penance was, I watched the tears and grief give way to hopefulness and resolve, and maybe a little bit of surprise.

"Will you do this thing," I asked him, "and tell no one, not even Effie? Because I'm counting on you. I can't make this thing work without you."

"I'll do it," he said, in a way that made me believe him. And when he stood up, he stood up straight in his old way, traveling all the way from his knees in a single motion. He had come back to himself.

"Thank you, Father," he said, pumping my hand. "Thank you."

"Umm," I said. He paused. "Would you please ask Mrs. Moses to step in for a moment?" He hesitated. "This isn't about you." He nodded, surprised, a little unsure, but he went out and she came in, closed the door, and sat down.

"You know, don't you," she said. I nodded. Her name had been on Frankie's list, too, and her photos in one of the boxes. She looked down at her hands, folded in her lap, and nearly whispered. "What happens now?"

I waited to answer until she raised her eyes. "Do you believe in God?" I asked.

~

When I heard the Cessna engine fire, I felt absolved, myself. I looked at my watch, and was amazed that it had only been about an hour since the marshal landed. Hard to believe he had his investigation concluded and was leaving so soon. For about fifteen

49

minutes the engine ran, warming up, and I sat at my desk, still too rattled to work, waiting for all my potential problems to fly away. Then the engine cut, and the silence rushed back, along with the knot in my stomach. Another twenty minutes went by as I sat frittering at my desk. Thanks to Frankie's notebook, I had meetings to schedule with what seemed like half the population of Chandelar. Instead, I kept imagining my own confession, absolution and jail time until Andy burst in through my front door calling my name.

"You're not going to believe this," he said. By the look on his face, I wasn't.

"What is it?" The calm place I'd got to while sorting out Mr. and Mrs. Moses now opened under me like a chasm. Feeling like I was about to fall out of my skin, I opened my mouth to say something like, "Did someone break in during the night and make off with critical evidence? Who could it be?"

"It's a will," said Andy. "Frankie made out a photographic will."

"Holographic," I said.

"Yeah, one of those. And he left everything to one person."

Something like a siren went off in my brain. I'd been to Frankie's and searched the place thoroughly. I didn't see a will. Frankie didn't actually seem like the will type. If he did leave a will, how could he have left it hidden so well that I didn't find it in several hours of tossing the place, and the marshal walks in and finds it in fifteen minutes? And it's not just a will, but a holographic will. It's so obviously in Frankie's handwriting that the marshal doesn't even bother to keep it a secret.

I could feel my spirits sinking. This was getting too complicated. My so-called good deed was in danger of obstructing a murder investigation. I had kept hoping the whole thing would just sort of gloss over, and that what I was trying to do wouldn't have an effect on what the marshal needed to do, but it kept not glossing over. And it left me with the feeling that I was just getting in deeper and deeper. Since when is it the priest's job to attempt to pull off a significant deception, however well meaning? What we call a 'lie' in the priest game.

That's when it seemed that the only thing left to do was to just go down and tell the marshal that I was there last night, that there was no will and that it's obviously a fake. A fake will that conveniently leaves everything to this one mystery person. *Boy*, I thought, *someone has some tough questions to answer about that.*

To Andy I said, "One person? Who?"

"Well that's the really funny part," said Andy. "You'll laugh. Looks like Frankie left about fifty thousand dollars cash, his whole place, and everything in it—to you!"

CHAPTER 7

"You never met Frankie Slick?" asked Marshal Jacobs. He smoothed his bristled mustache with a thumb and forefinger, and stared at me for a long, long moment.

I took a breath. "I'm sure we said hello or nodded at each other on the way out of the store or the Coffee Cup," I said. "It's a small town. But no, I never actually met the man."

"But he probably came to your church," said the marshal.

"If he had come to my church, then I would have met him," I said. The door opened and shut behind me, but I was on a roll. "Why is it so hard for you to believe that Frankie Slick left all his earthly belongings to a church? Maybe it was his way of repenting secret sins."

The marshal humphed. "Frankie didn't have any secret sins," he said, "and he didn't leave it to the church. He left it to you."

"Oh," I said, momentarily speechless, and that's when I turned and saw that it was Evangeline Williams who had come in.

I hadn't seen her since that day in my office, but she'd been on my mind so much I'd come to feel that I knew her and that we were friends, or at least friendly. We weren't. She hardly looked at me.

"Then I suppose you don't know Miss Williams, either," said the marshal.

"We've met," I said.

She flicked her eyes at me briefly, coldly. "Father," she said. And that was it. I've felt more warmth from river ice.

"Thanks for coming by, Father," said the marshal. I was dismissed again, and went out and walked home, feeling that somehow something had been lost from the day. It was as though one important light bulb had gone out in a room, leaving the light but taking the sparkle.

I sat at my kitchen table and missed my wife so much that I ached. These were the times, the talking-things-over times, the figuring-things-out times, the making-plans times, that had been our best. Now, without her, I had wandered from my straight and narrow path, to trying to do God's work by stealing, and being devious and prepared to lie. And then there was my so-called 'plan.' I could just imagine what Mary would have said about that.

I felt like I'd been sucker-punched by Evangeline Williams' unfriendliness at Frankie's. Something about first meeting her and thinking about her, and devising a plan to help her, had made the last couple of days pass lightly. Now, the cold and heavy darkness settled back around me, and a pressure of hopelessness made it almost hard to breathe.

I opened a fresh can of coffee and was filling the percolator basket when I heard the Cessna fire up again. I had convinced myself that he was just warming up the oil, so he could come back for another round, when I heard the plane taxi out onto the river ice and throttle up. He was gone; it was over for the moment.

Andy came through the door moments later. "Smelled the coffee," he said, and grabbed his mug from its hook. I filled it and he dropped into his usual chair at the kitchen table, sipped his coffee and stared at me deliberately. "You don't look very happy for a guy who just inherited a ton."

I shrugged. For once I couldn't think of a thing to say.

"Maybe you and a best friend could take off to Seattle for a week or two. Let's see, Seattle in November, temperature is probably about forty-five, which would make it about," he did a quick calculation, "seventy-five degrees warmer than it is here today. Like a heat wave. How does that sound, friend?"

I had to admit that just at this moment, it sounded pretty good.

"Or, we could be in Hawaii in three or four days. Temp there would be," more calculating, "let's see, seventy degrees there, so one-hundred-five degrees warmer than we are." He grinned. "I could go pack. I haven't been any place warm since I left Italy." He looked at his watch. "We're too late for the train but we could drive your new pickup to the airport in Fairbanks."

My new pickup. I had forgotten that part of it. Funny how God answers prayers.

I managed a smile. I knew he was trying to cheer me up. "It's not mine," I said. "None of it. I'm not sure why Frankie left me anything. I truly never met the man. And I never heard a single good thing about him. But even if he thought he was leaving it to me, he was leaving it to the church. I can't accept it—won't accept it. Besides, it only seems fair that money he made by victimizing the town, should go back to helping the people." I looked at Andy. "Don't you agree?"

He sighed theatrically. "I do," he said. "I was just kidding about Seattle and Hawaii. Sort of." He sipped his coffee for a long moment. "I'm just trying to figure out which part of getting all this stuff has you so far down in the dumps."

We heard two quick raps and the door opening, so I walked out into the front room to see who had come in. My face must have revealed something of my inner turmoil. It was Evangeline Williams, who gave me a small apologetic smile and quickly, lightly touched my cheek with her fingertips. It happened so quickly that later on, some part of me would wonder if it had happened at all.

"Evangeline," I said.

"Call me Evie."

"We're in the kitchen," I managed, guiding her past me. It would be an understatement to say I was stunned, after just having seen an entirely different side of her at Frankie's.

"Andy," I said, "do you know ...?"

"Ciao bella," said Andy, when he saw her. War or no, I think he left part of his heart somewhere along the Adriatic. He did know her and was obviously quite fond of her.

"Cousin," she said, patting him comfortably, even affectionately on the shoulder. And then, "Coffee? Is there enough for me?" She selected a robin's-egg-blue mug, one that Mary favored, filled it nearly up, topping it with about half a thimble of canned milk.

"I didn't know you two were cousins," I said. They laughed in tandem.

"You're forgetting where you are, and who we are," she said. "You probably don't have to go back too many generations with us Athabascans to find that everybody in the village is related. Our mothers were sisters," she added. "My mother died of TB, just a couple of weeks after Pearl Harbor, and then my father disappeared." Andy gave her a look.

"Disappeared into a bottle," she added.

"I can understand that," I said.

"Yeah," she said. "I'm sure you can. Anyway, they sent me to the mission school and I was okay at first, but then Andy went off to save Italy, and I just fell off the edge. Everybody I ever really cared about was gone. I cried myself to sleep every night for most of a year, until I began to talk about it as though it didn't hurt and I didn't care. Then, after a while, it *didn't* hurt as much, so I guess I assumed that it had something to do with being flip about it."

"I had to go," said Andy.

She grabbed his hand in both of hers. "I know you did. I was so proud of you. I am so proud of you. I just missed you, that's all, and I was afraid you wouldn't make it home and I'd be alone forever." Her eyes teared and she fanned at them with both hands.

She went on talking for a time about life in the mission school, working in the garden, carrying river salmon by the gills—one on each hand—up the narrow plank from the fish wheel. About standing at the fish-cleaning table with the other mission children, slitting and gutting the huge fish, selecting those to be smoked or dried, eating the red-orange eggs like candy and still smelling like fish at night in bed. My heart ached for the lonely little girl she'd been.

"What I don't understand," I said, "is how you got from the mission school to ..."

"Frankie?"

"He was such scum," said Andy.

"He wanted me," she said, and blushed. "I don't mean in the sex way. In fact, he used to tell me he had picked me out specially. He probably did; he was very deliberate. And by then, the sisters had too much of me being flip. So he paid one of my mother's half brothers to officially adopt me—which really just meant to come and sign me out of the school—I was fifteen at the time, and ..."

"And you went to live with him?"

"No," she said, "actually not. He bought a place for me just through that stand of trees behind his cabin. And when I was twenty-one he signed it over to me." She paused to look at Andy and then at me. "I don't have any excuses to make for Frankie," she said. "He wasn't one of the good guys. But in his way, he was good to me." She looked at Andy directly. "Okay?"

"Okay," he said, deliberately agreeable, and smiled at her. This was obviously ground they'd covered before, not always so amiably.

"Now," she said, "your turn. How does an earnest young man like yourself start out at St. Luke's Seminary in Sewanee, Tennessee, and end up in a little bitty village in Alaska, with people like us?"

I couldn't help but smile at her. I hadn't given her any of that information, not that it was secret or even particularly hard to find. Yet, somehow she'd managed. She radiated brightness, even into corners of my soul that hadn't seen much but dark for a while.

"I guess I was lucky," I said.

Evie took a sip from her mug and studied me over the rim. "Tell us how you met your wife."

"Mary," I said, and felt myself flinching. It had been a long time since I'd talked to anybody about her. But Evie wasn't to be put off.

"Do you remember the first time you saw her?" she asked. "The moment?"

"Oh yes," I said, "vividly."

"Well?" said Andy.

"Okay," I said. "I was in the middle of a fight."

"A fight?" they said.

"A match, actually. A boxing match. I'd just been knocked down hard, chimes ringing, brain whirling, and when I rolled my head to the right, there she was, just at eye level off the canvas. She looked like an angel, very pale and blond with impossibly blue eyes."

"Impossibly blue," said Andy to Evie, who shushed him.

She turned back to me. "Keep going."

"Well, I looked at her and she looked at me, and—I admit I was dopey—I was trying to figure out if she was an angel, and what that might be about, when she said something to me."

"And you could hear her?" asked Andy.

"No, it was way too noisy. I was fighting what they call a smoker in a little fight club in Chattanooga, against the all-city lightweight champ. It was very noisy."

"But she spoke to you?" said Evie.

"Yes. Well, she moved her mouth. I don't think she actually made a sound."

"But you knew what she said ..."

"It was very clear."

"Well what?" she demanded.

"She said 'Get up!' So I got up."

The two just looked at me. "So tell us what happened," said Evie. "I swear, you are harder to get a story out of than Andy. 'Tell me about Italy,' I say. 'Warm. Good coffee,' he says." She made a face. "You lost, right? You don't seem like the fighting type."

"He won," said Andy, looking at me. "Didn't you." It wasn't a question.

I took a sip of coffee, playing the moment. "Yeah," I said, "I won."

Evie turned abruptly to Andy. "How did you know? He's a priest for crissakes." She bobbed her head in my direction. "Oops. Sorry, Father."

"The way he moves," said Andy. "Like all his body parts sort of flow together. And, like he has a right to be wherever he happens to be standing. Priests usually walk into a place more like—shy." He laughed dismissively. "Or something like that."

"Tell us more," said Evie, and I guess I did. It was more than I'd had to say any time since Mary died. I told them about our life and her death and how it felt to go on alone. They listened, drank my coffee and made more, and asked the occasional question. Too soon it was dark again, approaching dinnertime, and the cousins bundled up and went out the door together, leaving me alone in the cabin with my memories—and a casserole from Mrs. Jimmy. It looked like it was made of canned Dinty Moore beef stew, with rice and noodles. I struck a wooden kitchen match and turned on the propane to heat my dinner.

~

There isn't much to do on a Friday night in Chandelar, Alaska. Those of us who don't go to either of the town's two bars, go to the movie at the Pioneer's of Alaska Hall, Igloo Number Nineteen, a 1901 vintage men's club, originally for white settlers.

But on a Friday night, a bright-eyed, bespectacled boy named Orie, gets there early enough to light a fire in the big barrel stove up front, to pop the popcorn, and get the first movie reel threaded into an antique projector. He's the only one who can keep it running. I've heard rumors of a pact with the devil.

Much of the town files in, kids to the hard benches near the screen where their front sides get roasted by proximity to the barrel stove at the same time as their backsides are still freezing. Adults sit on the hard chairs behind. The room starts out so cold that most of us leave our parkas on until about halfway through the movie when we all simultaneously realize we're sweltering and can't possibly wait for the reel change.

I sat in one of the last two empty seats about five rows back. The newsreel replayed the surrender of Japan. The crowd of mostly Athabascans hissed and booed the losers. "I already seen this one," someone muttered at my left elbow. "They get whipped!" I'd seen the feature, an old gangster picture, but my entertainment alternatives all seemed worse. Moments later, someone slipped into the vacant seat and tapped my knee. It was Evie.

Why was I so glad to see her? Was I glad to see her? Did I have a crush on another dying woman? I didn't even know her, and in spite of things I'd heard or not heard this afternoon, she was widely believed to have been working as a prostitute.

What would my parishioners think of their priest sitting next to a prostitute? Oh yeah, I know,

Jesus had friends who were prostitutes. And they crucified him.

I looked around the darkened hall and no one was watching me. They were watching George Raft and Humphrey Bogart wielding tommy guns. When the boy's dog died, I began to cry. It was the first time I'd been able to cry since Mary's death. I did what any man would do, pretended I wasn't crying. I sat up straight and didn't sob, but my nose ran and tears cascaded down my cheeks. Again the tap on my knee and Evie handed me a hanky, which I used. She slid her hand into mine and kept it there until I was finished crying. Then she gave it a squeeze and pulled her hand back. I didn't return the hanky.

Later, filing out, she said, "I cry at movies, too."

"Not gangster movies," I said. I admit I was feeling more than a little foolish.

When we paused on the wide, planked boardwalk out front, and I wanted to say anything but goodnight, she said, "Got any more of that coffee?"

"I do," I said. "Would you like to come over?" I was amazed at how easily the words rolled off my tongue, with just a little priming.

"I would. First, I'm going to go by my place and throw some wood in the stove and I'll meet you there, okay?"

I said okay and was halfway home before I realized that it was her way of not letting the whole town see us walk off together. News like that would have traveled, via the tundra telegraph, from one end of town to the other before we made it the two blocks to home.

There are no streetlights in Chandelar, which surprises visitors because it's dark so much of the time.

So, from down my block, I could see the light streaming out of my study window. "I'm home," I said, seeing the light. But actually I wasn't home and thought I remembered turning that light off. The closer I got, the more curious, until I stepped in through my wide-open front door.

My mistake. The wastebasket was empty because it had been turned upside down, along with everything else in the place. The sound of a footstep spun me around, fists up. It was Evie who joined me in the doorway to peer in at the mess.

"Bachelors!" she said.

CHAPTER 8

The entire contents of my cabin were now on the floor. The whole place was about ankle deep. Clothes, confidential papers from my filing cabinet, hundreds of books, and everything else I owned. I found myself drawn to only one thing, a photo of Mary and me taken at a small Tennessee lake in happier days. I found the frame and glass smashed to pieces, but the photo intact. I began to breathe again. It seemed that nothing else much mattered. Evie looked at me, looked at the photo.

"You okay?" she said, and when I nodded, went off down the hall on her own damage survey.

"Here's luck," she called from the kitchen. "They dumped the coffee but didn't scatter it." I heard sounds of scraping and then coffee making, and in a few minutes the comforting scent drifted down the hall into the jumble of my bedroom. They'd flipped the mattress off the bed and tipped over the dresser, but not until they pulled all the drawers and dumped them. Everything I owned was there for the digging through.

"Oh boy," she said, coming into the room behind me. "I guess we better start picking up in here."

"Why here?" I asked.

"So you have a place to sleep tonight." She gestured. "This looks like the usual place."

"You're right."

She tipped the dresser upright and began picking up drawers and inserting them. "Did they take anything," she asked. "Can you tell?"

I looked around. "Who knows?" I turned and walked back to my study. It wasn't big enough to overturn the desk, but again, all the drawers had been yanked and dumped. I could tell by the contents which drawer had been dumped in which pile. That's how I was able to turn over a desk calendar and pick up Teddy Moses' snub-nosed thirty-eight.

There came a low whistle of disbelief from the door. Evie had followed me, bearing steaming coffee mugs. "They didn't take the gun? This isn't kids."

I was already pretty sure it wasn't kids, just as I was also pretty sure what I thought they were looking for. "Wait here," I told her. "I've got to check the church building." I went out into the biting cold without taking the time to put my parka back on. Holding my breath I mounted the stairs and flicked on the overhead lights. No damage. Whoever it was, they hadn't looked here. And they hadn't discovered Frankie's ledger and photos wedged into the space behind the altar.

Although I was only out of the house a few minutes, Evie already had all the dresser drawers back in place and was folding the last of the clothing she picked up from the floor. She grabbed a pair of long johns she'd folded, and opened them, peering with one brown eye through perfectly aligned holes in front and back. "War wound?" she asked. "I'm not sure how you did this without hurting yourself."

"Well I …" I said, and then didn't know what else to say. The truth was, I had no idea how I'd ended up with perfectly lined-up holes in my drawers, and had never actually noticed them before.

I'd never seen anyone organize as aggressively as Evie. She lunged at disarray. Together we flopped the mattress back on its frame and by the time I'd recovered a pillow case and wrestled it onto my remaining, un-slashed pillow, she had applied sheets and blankets and was making professional-looking hospital corners to round out the job.

"You've done this before," I said.

She laughed. "Mission school," she said without slowing. She was gathering feathers and down from my gutted pillow into the pillowslip, likely for re-stuffing and mending later. Then she rehung a couple of pictures, bookended a cluster of books on my dresser top, and rounded up the remains of my Big Ben Jr. alarm clock from a corner where it had obviously been pitched. "This one didn't make it," she said, and swept up the bits of glass and odd feathers that were left.

"Some kids hated cleaning, but not me. I've always liked putting everything where it belongs, starting with a mess and finishing with everything organized, smooth and shiny. Too weird?"

"Nah," I said, "I get it. I like doing the same thing, only I try to do it with people's lives."

"Did you ever know Bishop Rowe?" she asked.

"Missed him," I said. "He had died and been replaced by Bishop Bentley—who recruited me to come to Alaska. Why?"

"He lived here sometimes, at the Mission, that is. This was his cabin. Did you know that? When they closed the Mission, they stuck this cabin on log skids and dragged it to town. I've already cleaned it dozens of times. When I look out this window, I always expect to see birch trees and the river. I miss seeing them through this window."

65

"What made you think of Bishop Rowe?"

"Oh, he said the same kind of thing that you did. Something about God putting people's lives in order, and him just helping out. I remember him sitting in your study, smoking a pipe and watching me dust books on the shelves. He seemed—holy!" She laughed self-consciously. "Funny, coming from me, huh?"

"You seem as holy as the next," I said. It bothered me that she had, probably as a child, learned to divide the world into who was holy, and who wasn't, including herself into the unholy group.

"Look," she said, "if you don't think this is too weird. I usually stay up most of the night." I must have given her a look. "I read books," she said defensively. "I just never have slept much. So why don't you crawl into bed—you look bushed—and let me just fuss with your stuff until I do get tired. Okay?"

I was tired, suddenly really tired. And I think, really discouraged. For a couple of days I'd been thinking how smart I was, with my plan to try to protect everybody and make everything right. Never mind that a man was dead, with his face eaten off, and a murderer still on the loose. I had felt nearly invincible. Now I just felt discouraged and very tired.

"If you're sure," I said, and sat down abruptly on the edge of my bed. She helped me pull my mukluks off, and then tiptoed quietly out the door as though I were already asleep. I climbed out of the rest of my outer clothing and slipped under my blanket, still wearing my longies. I knew I'd wake up freezing, sometime during the night, but was just too tired to care. "Goodnight," I called, but she didn't hear me. Or if she did hear me, she didn't answer. It didn't matter. I was already asleep.

Hours later I woke slightly from a dream that instantly fled. I wasn't cold. I now had an additional goose down sleeping bag covering me, and someone warm backed up against my body, on top of my covers but under the bag. It had been such a long time since I'd felt that enveloping warmth and closeness. She turned slightly, opened one eye to look at me, and sighed. "It's okay," she said softly, "it's just me. Go back to sleep."

With the curtain rods bent and twisted, and the curtains now neatly folded on my dresser top, the room was flooded with blue-white moonlight, diffused and patterned by the thick layer of frost on the insides of my window panes. It was nearly bright enough to read, so I had no trouble seeing Mary as she entered the room. I'd seen her this way before, wearing a white cotton nightie, coming back from the bathroom or from the kitchen, or letting the cat out, in those long-gone days when we had a cat and a normal life.

But instead of climbing back under the covers, Mary paused at the foot of the bed and gave me—and Evie—a long look. It was so really good to see her walking again and breathing on her own, looking healthy, happy and alive. She looked pink, even in the blue moonlight. It made me happy to see her so, even though I knew she wasn't. But I liked this way she looked, and I could feel it replace other graver memories. She shook her head a bit, smiled, and bending slightly at the waist, extended a forefinger to touch my big toe where it tented the blankets.

The next thing I knew, it was morning. I rolled over and looked for Mary, even though I knew I wouldn't find her. Even though I knew it had been a dream.

It was Evie who rolled over and looked at me. "Good morning," I said, smelling the warm perfume of her hair. She regarded me for a long moment and then closed her eyes. "Sleep more," she said faintly. But it was the last thing she murmured that made me shiver.

"Dreamed I saw a blond."

CHAPTER 9

That Sunday I decided to do a sermon on prayer. Frankly, it was one I'd given before, in seminary, and it had been received nicely on several "visiting preacher" outings. True, it was an easy one that needed little prep, but it also seemed to fit the moment.

Nobody questions prayer at the seminary. Everybody prays. They read prayers, they carefully compose prayers, they improvise prayers at picnics and pancake suppers, and nobody ever says, "I don't know why I'm doing this or if it really will work."

When Mary got sick, I prayed for her recovery. When she began to be paralyzed, I prayed for her to be able to move again. When she could no longer breathe on her own, I prayed for a miracle. Of all the favors I asked of God, the only one granted was the final one—that she be allowed to die.

But was that the answer to my prayer, or was it just what happened? As a priest, I would have to say it was what God decided. As a grieving husband, I was less sure.

So when I turned in the pulpit to deliver a sermon on prayer to my small congregation, I found myself shoving aside the sheaf of carefully typed, underlined, and notated script. Not today. My congregation of seventeen Athabascans and two whites—the public health nurse and her husband—looked up at me expectantly, confidently. With the exception of Evie, seated at the far back in a corner, they were all older than me, hair going to gray and faces that had become tanned and leathery with season after season of harsh weather. Most of them had rosy, apple cheeks and clusters of smile lines, deeply etched at the corners of their eyes. I found myself momentarily distracted by the realization that those who had maybe the least to smile about had faces most marked by smiles.

I had been prepared to tell them what St. Paul and others—who none of us had ever met, who had been dead a long time—believed about prayer. Instead, I decided to go out on a limb and tell them my own notions about prayer, and see where it got me.

"I don't really believe in most kinds of prayer," I began. My congregation is usually pretty impassive, but I saw several of them blink on this one. I was already imagining my explanation to the bishop.

"Most people," I said, "use prayer like a letter home for money: Dear Dad, dear Mom, send money, I'm in a jam. I've spent days, months, years getting myself into this jam, but now I need you to get me out of it quick, and if you do, I'll believe."

I got some smiles at that. Many of them had children or grandchildren away at the Indian schools. So they knew what those letters for cash were like. You had to wonder what their kids and grandkids could possibly be thinking. For the most part, my congregation lived on what they could shoot, catch, trap, or grow. When they needed something from the general store, they were likely to take in a stack of stretched-round beaver hides to barter. But when their children went off to the south—where people had actual cash—they somehow forgot that they'd scarcely ever, in their whole lives, seen their parents with any.

I went on. "So most of our prayers are about wants and needs. Give me these things and I'll believe." I looked at them all deliberately and they looked back. "This seems backward to me," I said, and I saw several nodding.

"It seems more reasonable—and to me the notion of a reasonable God seems reasonable—that we consider our thoughts as prayers. Most people agree that God knows our thoughts, so He knows who we are, where we are and what we need, at least as soon as we do. This was a notion that had hung me up as a youth. I had thoughts I wasn't comfortable with God knowing." They thought that was funny.

"Do you think God doesn't know we have impure thoughts?" I asked them. I know I can remember having a raft of impure thoughts the first time I met Mary. I didn't tell my congregation this. Even now, as a lonely bachelor, I'd managed one or two impure thoughts about Evie. I didn't tell them about that, either. And I avoided looking at her at this point. Standing in front of God and everyone, and especially her, I felt transparent, as though all my thoughts were clearly visible.

What I did tell them, and this was the point, of course, was that God created us, so He created our thoughts: the wholesome ones and the steamy ones. Our thoughts weren't strangers to Him. And I told them that what really interests God is how we ultimately sort out our thoughts, and what we do with them, or about them. That God judges us by what we do and what we say. Period. More nodding.

At the last, I told them about the power of prayer. "Prayer doesn't seem powerful, does it?" I asked them. "In fact, it seems kind of lonely and shy, like God hears one little prayer from over here and another from over there."

"But I have a theory," I told them, "that if you, and you, and you, and me—all of us—put our lonely, puny prayers together, the result is like a whole bunch of matches or candles that together, produce a big light, a ray of light that cuts through darkness and heals the sick and makes wrong things right. And that's why we're here in this room together, isn't it? Praying together. Praying for the same thing together. I'm convinced that can be powerful."

And that's when I realized I'd answered my own question.

~

Later, I asked Evie about "the blond."

"I don't know," she said, "I opened my eyes, saw a blond woman, closed them and went back to sleep."

"You saw a blond standing there and you went back to sleep?"

"Well, I knew I was dreaming. Besides, I've seen blonds before. And I was still tired. We … I was up late cleaning, remember?"

"What would you say," I asked her, "if I said that I had the same dream."

"That's definitely weird." She raised her eyebrows. "Maybe we weren't sleeping?"

"The only reasonable explanation is that we were sleeping," I said. "What other possible explanation could there be?"

She gave me nothing short of a look, a sort of piercing gaze with just one eyebrow raised. "Why does it have to be a reasonable explanation?" she asked. "Around here, a lot of people see people who are dead."

"You mean like … ghosts?"

"Oh, I get it," she said. "You can believe in something like God, who you've never seen, have you?"

"Well, no, not exactly, but ..."

Evie wrinkled her brow, and with an extended forefinger, punctuated her syllables in the air. "You're so busy seeing what you believe that you can't take the time to actually believe what you're seeing. I mean, I don't know how you can believe in a God you haven't seen, when you have trouble believing in a blond you actually have seen.

"That wasn't a blond," I said, "that was my wife, Mary."

"She looked blond to me."

"No, I mean, she was blond, but that was my wife."

She gave me a soft smile. "I know," she said, flipped up her parka hood and went out.

~

Bjorn "Big Scotty" Neilson sent for me. His Athabascan wife, a small, round, rosy-cheeked woman in a much-mended parka, came shyly tapping at my door, early. "He's dying," she whispered, eyes on her beaver-fringed mukluks.

I was only moments up, coffee barely on, dressed in longies and the woolen army overcoat that kept me alive one miserable French winter. Clutching her elbow, I was able to draw her into the room and quickly close the door. She was a presence as light on her feet as frost sparkles, and she seemed to not so much step in, as float in on a low-lying roil of ice fog.

"Should I come right now," I asked, "or in one hour?"

"One hour," she said, and risked meeting my eyes for a sliver of a heartbeat. Warm tears broke a chilly trail from each eye down the softly mounded landscape of her face to her chin, which was nearly concealed behind her frosty parka ruff.

"Will the Great God take him this time?"

"The Great God doesn't tell me His secrets," I told her. "But I'll come and pray with him."

"In one hour."

"Tell him I'll be there."

The first time she came, well before sunup on a frosty morning, I'd dressed in a spasm, thrown myself into my parka, shut off the gas under the half-perked coffee and set off at a trot with my prayer book and a small, Mennen aftershave bottle of holy oil. Tiny Mrs. Neilson, not nearly five feet tall, almost trotted down the icy skim of the snow-packed street in my wake.

But Big Scotty turned up near death just about once a month, neatly coinciding with the arrival of his government check, and a brush with the most rotgut whisky, probably locally distilled, that he could find.

So I'd turned up and prayed over him, talked a little, and listened a lot to a lonely man who'd grown old, unexpectedly to himself. One day there was more behind him than before him, and it made him sad.

"What do you think, Padre. Do you think I'm dying?"

"I'm afraid I think you're a little drunk."

He gave me a look. "If you were dying, don't you think you'd want to be a little drunk?"

He had a point.

CHAPTER 10

We were crowded around a table in the Coffee Cup Café, under the bright red neon of a saucer and a steamy cup of joe. Here in Chandelar, the Coffee Cup is home to the heavy, bottomless mug of coffee for a quarter, and for seventy-five cents, a stack of sourdough pancakes, served with your choice of nearly black molasses, sweet fireweed honey, or summer-canned strawberry jam. It was dark outside. The sun wouldn't rise for another couple of hours, but with the large picture window a frozen sheet of ice, we couldn't see out anyway. For a quarter, we had three tunes on the jukebox. One of them was Patti Page, who was singing her new hit, Tennessee Waltz, which—even though it's not about Tennessee—still managed to make me a little homesick for Sewanee.

"So," said Andy, forking a last mouthful of pancakes, lowering his voice and leaning across the red-and-white checkered oilcloth, "when we gonna test drive that new pickup of yours? Just you and me."

"Me too," said Jerry, turning from a conversation about moose guns. "I'm in."

"I will go too." It was the fourth member of our Saturday morning 'meeting,' William Stolz, custodian at the school, just arriving. He pulled back the heavy chrome chair and slid into place while holding up his coffee mug for a fill. Rosie Jimmy, the waitress managed to pour the mug full while passing, not stopping and not spilling a drop. She had waffled long johns showing beneath her pink waitress outfit, and caribou mukluks on her feet. As William cautiously sipped, the hot steam fogged his rimless spectacles, and he wiped his drippy nose on the back of one sleeve.

"We could go down to Clear," he said. "I've heard there's a fresh supply of that skookum three-quarter-inch plywood for the hauling." He turned to me. "And you have a pickup truck."

"Well…" I said, with the intention of explaining why the plywood trip couldn't happen. But the sight of them, rimming the table, leaning forward in a hushed, expectant way, made all the rather lame excuses I might have made sound … lame. They were right. Somehow, it was my pickup truck. Well, it was the church's pickup truck, entrusted to my care. And these, for the most part were my parishioners. And they were entitled, as much or more than any citizen in the country, to the U.S. Government's cast off, scarcely-used plywood.

"Okay," I said. "We'll do it." Their joint exclamation of pleasure was loud enough that people at the other tables lifted their heads and swiveled around to see what we were up to. We hunkered down, happy, all thoughts on free plywood.

"God! This coffee is good," said William, and signaled with his mug for another round.

"No it isn't," said Andy. "This stuff is swill."

"Cheez," said Jerry, "here he goes again. 'Eye-talian coffee is better than any other coffee in the world.' But I'm trying to tell him, how can it be any darn good if it doesn't even come in a can?"

"In Italy, they roast the coffee themselves," said Andy. "And you sit in a little café on the sidewalk, while beautiful Italians walk by as you sip. And the flavor of the coffee fills your mouth. It's like the flavor explodes!" he said, coming back from that other place and slamming his open hand on the tabletop.

"Ciao bella," he called out to Rosie, the Italian sounding unfamiliar on an Athabascan who tended to talk with his jaw stiff and teeth somewhat clenched. But it wasn't wasted on Rosie who came on the run with another round of coffee 'from the red can that means good taste.'

~

Turns out, the pickup was low on fuel.

"Damn that cheapskate Frankie," said Jerry, "to go and die on us with the tank empty." Maybe it was high spirits over our trip, but we all laughed and took turns out on the dock at Standard Oil, hand-pumping the fuel into the new Ford's tank.

The truck had started in a heartbeat, just like it was ready to go and thought the trip a good idea. Andy and Jerry volunteered to sit in the unprotected bed, but it was twenty miles out to Clear, at about thirty below, and we ended up with the four of us jammed into what quickly became a steamy cab.

"It reminds me of the war," said William. "It was bitterly cold. We were far too many stuffed in front with the driver. Some in the back froze to death."

"No freezing where I was," said Andy, "on the Italian coast. Nobody freezing there!"

"I nearly froze right here," said Jerry, who had been too young for the war. That, and an early bout with TB had kept him in Chandelar.

"It was cold in France," I said, "but I don't think I heard of anybody freezing."

77

"I was in Stalingrad where the frozen bodies were stacked up like cordwood," said William. No one commented. We had all grown accustomed to William's particularly grim war memories.

"I won't forget the first time I saw the Mediterranean," said Andy. "It was kind of a blue-green color like I never seen before. And warm! You could walk right in without worrying about your nuts freezing solid and falling off."

"I had this whole damn place to myself," said Jerry. "Sorry, Father. Those days, with Andy gone, I could have any girlfriend in the whole valley. Why'd you come back?" he asked suddenly then laughed uproariously.

"Couldn't get any goddamn Krauts to shoot me," said Andy, along with the obligatory, "Sorry, Father."

We should get out more often, I was thinking. This was the first time I'd been able to not think about Frankie Slick, about who killed him, and who trashed my place. Then, with a bit of a shock, I also realized that I'd gone much of the day without thinking about Mary. I felt both happy and a little disloyal at the same time.

It took nearly an hour of slogging down a snow-drifted road to reach the new government station. As we rounded the last corner, I must have gasped. Radar screens, as big as football fields, aimed off toward the Soviets, 'listening' for sounds of the big attack everyone seemed to expect. Once a month all the school children in the nation would quickly climb under their desks and cover their heads, in practice for the attack. Ten years ago, Russians were our allies. *Attack us?* I wondered? *Why?*

It didn't take long to find the dump, and to find out the stories had been true. There were sixteen sheets of nearly new three-quarter-inch plywood for the taking.

"What a haul!" said Andy.

"New floor in my cabin," said Jerry.

"It is a great day," said William, and insisted on lining us all up, just so, for pictures. He fooled around and fooled around, posing us with the new pickup and the plywood all loaded, even producing a pocket-sized folding tripod from his parka, so he could set some gadget and join us for shot after shot from every conceivable angle. When he finally called for one more shot his models staged a rebellion, whooping and laughing, pelting him with feathery pieces of snow crust, since the drifted mounds of snow were far too fine and dry to pack into anything like a snowball.

Then we piled back into the cab, and began our high-spirited, steamy journey home. "I haven't been this steamy in a cab since Thelma Charlie from Tanacross," said Jerry. "Remember her, Andy?"

"I remember you tried to dance too close at the Civic Center and she slapped you," laughed Andy.

"She slapped you?" said William, a bit amazed. "Which reminds me of a waitress with a hand grenade in a little town in Chechnya," he said.

CHAPTER 11

A five a.m. call from the public health nurse got me up and out to baptize a very sick infant. Then, lingering to drink a cup of tea, I watched the child's fever break and temperature begin to fall. Shaking out the thermometer, the nurse's eyes met mine. "I can't explain this," she said.

"Sometimes it works this way," I said. But I was thinking of Mary and how sometimes it doesn't work this way. And I couldn't help wondering what makes the difference. Or why there is a difference.

On my way home, walking up my street, I saw the thin plume of wood smoke rising from my chimney in the windless dawn. It told me there was someone making himself comfortable in my cabin, building a fire in my stove. I was pretty sure it wasn't me.

"Hello?" I called cautiously, opening the front door a crack and placing my foot against it. I wasn't taking chances after my last unexpected visitor.

"Come in, my boy, come in." It was a voice I knew well, along with the aromatic, cherry scent of pipe tobacco. He rose from my sofa where he'd been reading the latest edition of the *Saturday Evening Post*, pipe smoke wreathing his head. It was Father Bernard Mendelson of St. Mary's Mission, south of here on the Tanana, well in his seventies now but an Alaskan legend.

He wasn't tall, maybe five foot six, with pewter-colored hair cut monk-like. Out on the trail, his unruly silver eyebrows would condense with moisture from his breath and freeze stiff and white, partly concealing a pair of piercing blue eyes, now slightly enlarged behind rimless reading glasses. Even in the Bush he wore a white clerical collar, black shirt and largish silver cross on a braided cord around his neck.

"Walked in," he said, seeing me check my watch for the train's arrival times. "Started about four. I'm headed to Fairbanks but the train hit a moose, and so it's running about two hours behind."

"Coffee?" I asked.

"Oh, lovely," he replied. "And I couldn't help but notice that you have several eggs in your cooler, and I wonder if I might have one of those fried. I haven't had a fried egg in ever so long."

"It's better than that," I said.

"Better?"

"Canadian bacon. A bit left from a can my friend Andy brought by."

"Ah, God bless Andy," said Father Mendelson, making the sign of the cross over his chest, serious about blessings.

Later, wiping away the absolute last trace of egg yolk with one of my leftover pancakes, he fixed me in his steady gaze. "It's about six months now, isn't it?"

"Starting the sixth," I said. "I stepped off the train on July one."

"And," he looked around the room, "how is it going?"

"It's going well, I think. Yes, I would say it's going well."

"But you're not eating," he said.

"I wasn't for awhile. Some of the ladies have been bringing food in. Afraid I'm not much of a cook." The old priest smiled and nodded.

"That happened to me after Ruth died," he said. I had heard the stories. He had come home from a dogsled circuit of some of the winter missions, to find his wife of forty years not only dead, but frozen in her rocking chair. There was a note in her hand.

'I may not be here when you get home,' she had written.

The two of us sat for long moments in companionable silence, hearing only the tick of the Seth Thomas mantle clock, and the low murmur of crackle from the woodstove. I'd built few fires since the installation of my oil furnace, and found myself wondering why. The yellow flicker of fire and faint, resinous perfume of its smoke gave life and comfort to an otherwise empty room—a center. Certainly I had never found myself, of an evening, sitting and staring thoughtfully into the grate of my oil furnace.

"The Arctic," he said, appearing to choose his words carefully, "is a hard place to be lonely. Some men drink; some go mad. Some see things," he said, and fixed me with his deliberate gaze.

"Things like?" I said. But I was pretty sure I knew where he was going with this.

He seemed to focus on me a bit more sharply. "Spirits," he said. "Some people, especially lonely people, imagine they see the departed. Talk to them, even."

"Ahhh," I said. He nodded, as though we had achieved a breakthrough.

"The natives freely admit they see spirits," he said, "and they talk to them as well as listen to them.

But the natives are simpler souls with superstitions left from other beliefs and their own ancient culture. They are unsophisticated about their beliefs."

"Father," I said, "isn't belief, by definition unsophisticated? We either do believe or we don't?"

"Well," he said. "Yes." He shifted in his chair, as though not quite comfortable.

"When I was a child, people used to say 'seeing is believing.' It was so clean and simple. But now I've seen so much, and some of the things I've seen are impossible to explain. If I hadn't seen them myself, would be difficult to believe. So at my age, 'belief' is complicated. It's certainly not for the timid."

"So," I said, "a man might fancy he sees these spirits out of nothing more than loneliness?"

"Quite right," he said, and began to fiddle with his pipe, which had gone out again.

"And so," I said, "you've come to warn me about these visions." He nodded emphatically.

"The Bishop asked me to stop in." He shifted again and began to dig in his pockets.

"The Bishop is concerned that I might see visions?" He nodded, still searching pocket-to-pocket.

"I was very lonely after Ruth died," he said at length, carving the remains of a blackened plug of tobacco out of his pipe with a small pocketknife. "Very lonely. And I think that's why I saw her. She came to me in a dream. I had preached a sermon, come home and had a little lunch, then laid down for a short nap, and there she was."

"It's you, I said, but she didn't answer me. She said, 'Wake up now and go to the Jacobsons.' And behind her, as if in an adjoining room, I heard heartbreaking sounds of screaming and crying. It was all very disturbing."

"What did you do?" I asked him.

He looked at me as if surprised. "I got up," he said, "put on my parka, and jogged the several blocks to the Jacobson cabin. They were an old Norwegian couple, well in their eighties, and as I jogged, I rehearsed what I might say to them to explain my foolish mission. But when I walked up on the porch, I heard screaming and sobbing, so I pushed my way in. The old man had let the fire go out in his iron stove, to make repairs, and it had tipped on him, pinning him against the wall, slowly compressing his chest so that he couldn't breathe. He had just a few moments before he would lose consciousness—forever."

"What did you do?"

"I was unable to tip the stove off, using my own strength, but seized a length of iron pipe and levered the weight up off him so he could be pulled free."

"You saved him," I said.

"Yes indeed. But it was close, very close, and if it hadn't been for Ruth …"

"The vision of Ruth," I said.

"Yes."

"So," I said, "I'm not sure if I get this. You've come to tell me that I might see these visions because I'm here in the north, lonely, but that I should ignore them?"

The old man was nodding, agreeing, but then stopped abruptly. "Ignore them at your peril," he said. "The ones you need are the ones that come."

CHAPTER 12

As the next couple of weeks passed, I worked my way down Frankie's blackmail list. It was almost always the same. I'd call the victim on the phone, or send word that I needed to speak to them about some 'government' thing. Did it fool anybody? I don't know. Most of his victims were men, but there were a few women, too. And they weren't all local. He had victims all over the territory.

The married principal at the tiny high school— just twelve students—had been sleeping with the high school secretary. It would be an automatic dismissal and likely a beating for both at the hands of her husband, if discovered. The administrator of the Ice Pool betting fund had been skimming thousands of dollars of local salary. He could easily be shot for this. Frankie even knew the total amount of funds taken. Husbands had been unfaithful with other men's wives or with prostitutes—never named—and they were making regular payments of cash, pelts of beaver or wolverine, guns, or anything else of value they might be squeezed for. And they'd have been paying forever. Of course, every one of them was a suspect in Frankie's murder.

I'd contact the ones I could, show them into my office and close the door, and then show each his—or her—name on the ledger, with other names blocked out. Some would cry; some would curse. One man asked me how much payment I would be expecting. All were a bit dumbfounded when I told them.

Each in turn, confessed the sin, vowed to change for the better, and was absolved. They then went next door to the church to begin the specific praying I had requested as their penance. It looked to me like most went joyfully.

Only one refused to confess his sin, and refused to be absolved: Andy. I had known his name would be on the list when I found what had to be his sniper rifle chained with the others to a bolt on Frankie's gun wall. There wouldn't be two such rifles in the Tanana Valley. In the ledger, Andy's name was visible, but his 'sin' had been blacked out.

"Can't do it, Father," said Andy, meeting my eyes. "I admit that Frankie had something on me, that's why I had to turn over the rifle. That was it, full payment. But I don't intend to confess it, and won't be absolved."

He studied his hands for a moment. "It's a very good offer. I appreciate what you're trying to do for me. For everybody. And I understand that this is priest business. But I don't need you as my priest on this." He raised his eyes to meet mine. "I need you as my friend."

It was a long moment. I confess I was a bit miffed that, of the lot, he was going to muck up my prayer plan. I had to shake that crazy notion out of my head. Here was a man I knew to be a good man, regardless of Frankie Slick, asking for my understanding, friendship, and trust. Although I didn't exactly 'get' what was going on, I got that this was a critical moment between us and instead of answering, stuck out my hand.

We shook on it, and I retrieved his rifle from behind the study door. He worked the bolt, squinted through the high-powered telescopic sight and smiled. Then he thanked me and went out. As I watched him go, I wondered what he could possibly have done to get sideways with Frankie Slick. And I wondered if it could really all be settled so reasonably and never heard of again.

I guess I didn't think so.

CHAPTER 13

Courtesy of Frankie, the church's new gray Ford truck, with snow tires all around, swished nearly silently through a good eight inches of untracked snow. I drove up a lane framed in white paper birches—stark in this season—to the large, old, somewhat foreboding building that had once been the home of almost everybody I knew in Chandelar: the old mission school.

If I were a person who spooked easily, and I'm usually not, I admit I'd be spooked here. Like the ancient explorers' maps that read, 'Here there be tygers,' a map to the old mission, just a mile out of Chandelar, might read, 'here there be restless spirits and dark, possibly dangerous secrets.'

Built early in the century and originally a log structure, it had later been bevel-sided and painted the color of creamed coffee, with darker coffee trim. From a large three-story central core, two identical wings— likely one for boys and the other for girls—jutted off one side with a space in between. On the corrugated tin roof, were several large, old, cone-shaped sheet metal ventilators, and from the darkened, frosty windows, I imagined the lonely eyes of fifty years of displaced Athabascan children.

From about 1905 through the influenza epidemic of 1918, all the way up until just a couple of years before my arrival, Indian children had been sent here. While some came for education, homeless, parentless, sometimes so-called incorrigible children were sent here as well.

Looking back, it was easy to feel sorry for them. Fact was, in their day, they were the lucky ones. They got three meals a day, lessons, a simple trade—like carpentry or sewing—and protection from bad things that happen to parentless children, or children of alcoholics.

I had inherited an immense heavy ring of keys with my new job that didn't unlock anything I'd been able to find at the church in town. But four or five tries here got me in the front door, which creaked and crackled open in the minus-thirty-five degree cold. I closed the door behind me with an effort, reluctantly, not wanting to separate myself from the bright sun on snow, giving myself wholly over to the secrets of this now dark place.

There's a story, a famous story in the Alaska Missions, of a deaconess here who one night put herself between a drunken man and a young girl he wanted. As the story goes, the man who had lived here himself as a child, relented and began to cry and beg forgiveness from his old teacher. And she forgave him. But the strain had been too much and she collapsed that night and died. There were those who had known her who said they still saw her here.

I thought of her now as my warm breath hung and shifted in the chill half-light. It didn't take any imagination at all to see a thin, bespectacled, women in black deaconess habit staring back at me. What would she tell me? I listened hard but the silence was complete.

From my pocket, a small flashlight helped me down a long, dark corridor, strewn with debris. The air was stale with the scent of old clothes, rodents, dampness, and time. In the gloom, I almost missed a line of framed black-and-white images, mostly of children. There was Evie, first as a young girl and then a young teen with two others. She was already alluring. The three faced the camera, smiling slightly, shiny dark hair combed straight back and tied, dress hems long, with a kind of sailor collar that had been popular decades before.

There was Jerry, about eleven, grinning his crooked grin. There Andy, Jerry and another boy, arms roughly about each other's shoulders. It was Frankie! Having recently pulled frosty Frankie from the snow bank, these smiles—on that long ago, birch-filled summer day—were haunting. In one more photo, down at the very end, taller, bulkier Jerry stood with short, slight Frankie. Frankie's chest was out and head up, like he was a tough guy, with Jerry standing slightly behind, on guard.

The kitchen still hung with an assortment of stainless spoons, whisks, and an impressive array of institutional-sized kettles. Soup has always been a popular way to make food stretch. I pulled one kettle aside for summer Bible school Kool-Aid. Cabinet doors ajar, a few bags and boxes of things like flour, oatmeal, and baking soda lay torn and dumped by rodents. One heavy, restaurant-style coffee mug lay on its side on an old linoleum countertop, edged in chrome. I turned the mug upright. A stain of coffee remained in the bottom. I walked on, then walked back and slipped the mug into my parka pocket. It would be the only one of my collection not chipped.

I shivered, not from cold, and looked over my shoulder. What did I expect? I expected nothing and it was exactly nothing that I found. But why did it seem so scary? The frozen floor cracked under my feet as I slowly stepped along another hall. Strewn, broken toys gave way to randomly stacked and scattered books. Doorknobs, in this place of small children, were nearly a foot lower than usual on the paneled doors.

An office. I pushed open a door of dark wood and found myself face-to-face with a large, framed photograph of Alaska's first Episcopal missionary bishop, Peter Trimble Rowe. Holding a pipe with a curved stem, he seemed to be regarding me intently, as if to ask, 'What are you doing here?' And, 'Why are you covering up details of a murder?' I had to admit, I didn't have a convincing answer to either question.

Up the creaky stairs I went, along a corridor patterned with rectangles of frost-subdued sunlight, searching for what? I wasn't sure. Out of the corner of my eye I saw a fleeting shape. "Mary?" I said softly. But no one answered. Another movement, I turned my head again, and shivered, the hairs on the back of my neck rising, as the corridor thickened with shapes of raucous children, hearing their laugher, their called-out names as they ran past and through me. The whole thing lasted just for a second, leaving me alone again.

First seeing Mary and now these children, some likely dead for decades, left me trembling and weak-kneed.

"Am I seeing ghosts ... losing my mind?" I said to the silence. It's all well and good that the prayer book talks of the Holy Ghost. Are these the unholy ghosts? They didn't seem unholy. Maybe ghosts are nothing more than a drifting sense of time, like a layer of life that shifts, just for a heartbeat, offering the

91

unexpected glimpse. Father Mendelson said you see the ones you need. But why here, why now, why me?

Or was this all just the plain old garden-variety guilt of a priest who moves to a strange and lonely place, is attracted to a woman who seems morally uncertain, and begins to shape his beliefs and behavior to suit his own needs and desires?

I was still thinking of Evie as I went out the front door and banged it shut. I locked it, and trudged back to the truck with my salvaged Kool-Aid kettle and unwashed coffee mug, glad to leave the shadows and darkness behind.

Morally uncertain? Was she? In the intense, blue-white light of an arctic midday, I didn't think so. Was I morally uncertain? Maybe a little. But then, covering up a murder, blackmail, child pornography, and whatever else, was bound to leave a priest feeling out a bit on thin ice.

Circling the truck, I put the mug in the kettle, and the kettle in the snow-mounded truck bed. Which is how I came to see the footprints, neatly concealed in my tire treads, mukluked feet that followed me here and then went away.

CHAPTER 14

Monday morning at eight, I was just pouring myself a cup of coffee, planning my day, when trouble came calling.

I opened my frost-rimmed front door to find a man in stateside clothing—a brown woolen overcoat, black galoshes with snaps, black leather gloves, and an olive-drab, military-issue hat with earflaps. He appeared, something like Marley's ghost, from an ice cloud of moisture and motor exhaust. He'd left his late-forties, Army-colored Ford sedan idling in the street. It had 'U.S. Government' stenciled in white on the front door.

"Come in," I said. But by then he was already standing in my front room with the door closed behind him.

"Father Hardy," he said, "I'm here on U.S. Government business."

"Swell," I said. "Who are you?"

"Masterson," he said. "Special agent, attached to DEW Line, Clear." He hesitated, his eyes sliding sideways.

Removing his hat revealed a blondish, waxed, precise flattop. His face had a pasty quality with gray circles around the eyes, and he had an anxious kind of vibration to him—maybe desperation—that seemed to be driving him. Some people you have to be around a while to not be comfortable with. This guy made me edgy right away.

From his inside shirt pocket, he pulled heavy-rimmed black glasses. Slipping them on, he examined me carefully. From my view, his murky eyes appeared slightly, optically enlarged and almost twitchy, like he'd had way too much coffee. "Your government needs your help," he said.

"My government needs my help?" I said back to him. I couldn't help remembering that the last time my government needed my help I'd ended up in France, in olive drab, being shot at.

"That's why I'm here," he said.

"Right," I said. "And what kind of help is it that my government needs?"

For whatever reason, he seemed suddenly reluctant to tell me. Instead, he eyed my coffee mug, rubbed his bluish hands together, and shivered. "Got any more of that coffee?"

"Right," I said again, and led him to the kitchen, where he dropped his gear on a chair and selected a mug. Five teaspoons of sugar. "This all you got?" he asked, eyeing the canned milk. I nodded. He poured, stirred, sipped. "Now this is great coffee," he said without meaning it. Then he looked at me significantly.

"First," he said, "I need everything you've got on Franklin Delano Nicolai."

"You've wasted your time," I said. "Never heard of him and so I have nothing on him."

"AKA Frankie Slick," he said.

Ah, that was it. I couldn't help laughing, which didn't please him. "What could my government possibly care about Frankie Slick?" Masterson sat up straighter and turned up the intensity on what was supposed to be his hard look. It wasn't working. He looked more nearly pathetic.

"I don't think you understand," he said, and I think we both heard the quaver in his voice. "This is government business. I ask the questions, you provide the answers."

"I don't have any answers," I said. "I never met the man."

"Well," he said, "for starters, do you know where I can find him?" It seemed an odd question since I just said I'd never met him.

"As a matter of fact, you've asked one of the only questions I can answer. I know exactly where he is."

"I thought so," he said. "That's better." He seemed pleased with himself, but I noticed his coffee mug shaking. "Now we're getting somewhere."

About a half hour later we were back in my kitchen. Masterson, for his earnest attempt at hard-case demeanor, was still ashen from his first brush with faceless Frankie Slick. One look and he'd been out the door, sick behind the meat shed.

"You didn't tell me he'd been ..." he faltered.

I looked at him. "You said you were asking the questions. You didn't ask me that one."

He laughed weakly, his face still a little gray. "Okay," he said. He waved dismissively. "What else do you know that I haven't asked?"

"I know that someone shot him. That's about it. I went out with a couple of mushers, the ones who found him, and we brought him in. Someone broke into the shed, turned out his pockets looking for something and took the mousetraps. You saw what happened."

"Boy did I," he muttered. "What I don't get," he said, "is how you came to inherit."

That stopped me. "You knew I inherited," I said, thinking out loud. "So it's safe to assume you already knew he was dead. And that means you probably already knew where the body was; you just needed me to get you in." He eyed me blankly, then turned to stare out the still-dark window. "So how did you know I inherited?"

"It's common knowledge," he blustered. "Street talk."

I confess I stared at him. Around whites, Athabascans were the most private people I'd ever met. It was unlikely anyone in Chandelar, that I knew—which was just about everyone—would stop for even a minute to gossip with this obviously strung-out cheechako.

"We think Mr. Nicolai ... Mr. Slick ... was involved in something," he said, and raised one eyebrow with significance.

"Who would 'we' be?" I asked.

"Us," he said. "Your government. Which is why I need to get a look inside of that safe."

I hadn't mentioned a safe to anyone and certainly didn't believe that it was common knowledge. Andy told me that Slick came to his house to collect the sniper rifle, and they made the deal in the truck. Frankie pointedly didn't want people in his cabin.

"Time for you to go," I said, handing him his things and herding him toward the door. "I've got to see to my parishioners."

"But what about the safe," he said, and I could feel the desperation in him, rising.

96

"What safe?" I asked. His mouth moved, but no sound came out.

He pulled off his glasses and jammed them impatiently into his shirt pocket. "What about helping your country?" he demanded, his voice rising. "I'm sorry," he said, without looking it. "I'm going to have to report back to my people that you're unwilling to help."

I knew he was lying and sensed he was desperate, but it didn't help. It had been a long time, not the war—probably junior high school—since I had felt like I was feeling now: angry and wanting to punch someone. I could feel it start somewhere near my gut and rise like heat. The problem at the moment was that it felt good, and I really wanted to punch him.

"Were you in the war?" I asked him.

"Well … no, not exactly."

"How can you be 'not exactly' in the war?"

"Farming," he said. "Essential services."

"While you were farming, I was in France. I was one of those guys with the red cross on my helmet that the enemy used for target practice. And when they got too close, I got to stand out on the line and try to defend myself with a sidearm, while my friends were dying."

A quick knock on the door, it opened, and there was Evie, suddenly standing between us.

She looked at us, from one to the other, her eyes widening as they met mine. "Come to clean, Father," she said, in what I now recognized as her "village" voice. "Now a good time?"

"Sure. Good time," I said, realizing I'd been rescued, and the heat fled. Still, I nearly pushed the man, helping him out the door.

"On the battlefield, Mr. Masterson. That's how I've been helping my government. Tell them that."

CHAPTER 15

"I have a bad feeling about this," said Evie. She had already said it several times. We were sitting at my kitchen table, sipping steaming coffee. She held her mug in both hands as she sipped, her brow furrowed and her brown eyes serious. "We need to tell Andy about Masterson," she said.

As if on cue, there came a quick knock, the creak of the front door opening on frozen hinges, and Andy's voice. "I smell coffee," he called out. By the time he'd shed his parka and mitts and joined us in the kitchen, Evie had his coffee poured and waiting for him.

He was surprised to see Evie. In fact, the sight of her stopped him in the doorway. He looked deliberately at her, then at me, then moved smoothly to a stool by simply walking over it and sitting down. He looked at each of us again, intently, then said, "Aha!"

Evie blushed, a soft pink suffusing her face in a way that made her suddenly, incredibly lovely. Andy and I must have both been staring. "Stop it, you two," she said, and shaded her upper face with her hand until the glow subsided.

"Good coffee," said Andy changing the subject. "Mmm. Love that coffee from the big red can. So, what did I miss?"

The abrupt return to thinking about Masterson must have shown clearly on our faces. "Uh- oh," he said, "I did miss something. Let's have it."

So we went back over the Masterson visit, from him pushing his way in my door, clear through to me wanting to punch him just as Evie arrived.

"Shoulda punched him," said Andy.

"Don't be such a 'guy,' Andy," said Evie. "I'm worried about this and you should be too."

Andy swallowed a sip of his coffee and made a bad face. He sat for a moment. "You don't even know if this guy is on the level," he said. "Seems like he was just fishing for information. How bad can that be?"

"He's an outsider," said Evie, "the worst kind of cheechako. He shows up out of the blue, he knows about Frankie, knows about the will, knows about the safe. Since when did anything Frankie had to do with involve the army or the government? You know what," she said, "it's starting to scare the heck out of me."

Again the door. A firm, businesslike knock, all of us startling the same, Andy half rising from his stool. "Halloo," called a voice, a familiar voice.

"Back here, William," I called out to him. We waited while he shuffled himself out of his long parka, mitts and stocking cap, even going back out into the vestibule once to kick snow out of the deep treads of his snow boots.

He came into the kitchen, blotting his dripping nose on his sweater sleeve. "Ah, coffee," he exclaimed in a happy voice. This time Andy poured, shoveling sugar—three heaping teaspoons—and a healthy splash of the cold, nearly viscous canned milk—just the way he liked it. And soon William was perched on his stool, long, bluish hands wrapped around a steaming mug, looking from face to face expectantly. "Something has happened?" he said, his brows raised and his pale eyes curious behind rimless lenses. In a small, isolated Alaska town, in deep winter, where sometimes nothing happened for weeks or months, the expectation of news could be palpable. "Tell me," he said. "Tell me everything!"

So I started from the beginning and told about the visit from the man calling himself Masterson, Evie picking up the story from her perspective, possibly overstating the punching-in-the-nose part. In her telling, it was only her quick, active intervention that kept me from decking the man.

"That's not how it happened," I protested. She smiled.

"But you've got to admit it makes a better story," she said.

"I have never seen this man about town, or at Clear," said William. "And I go down there most Thursdays to play pool and take money from servicemen and technicians who are working there. I am sure I would recognize this one."

"You can get on the base to play pool?" asked Andy.

"I told them I was a veteran," said William. He smiled. "I told them it was my constitutional right as a citizen and a veteran to play pool on military bases throughout the free world."

"And they bought it?" I said.

"Not really," he said. "Their security isn't very good. They let me on once and I pretended to lose, so they invited me back." William climbed off his stool to grab the coffee pot, topped off each of the mugs and then sat down again, looking thoughtful. "I agree with

Evie," he said finally, seriously, staring into his coffee. "This man, Masterson, is a stranger. An outsider. And yet, he knows everything."

"This is so much more than Frankie bleeding lunch money from friends and relatives who've been careless," said Evie.

"Yes," said William. "This feels dangerous."

"But this is Frankie. Was Frankie," said Andy. "If he was ever dangerous, now he's dead. Hard to be dangerous when you're dead."

"I'm beginning to think it wasn't Frankie who was dangerous," I said. "The trouble didn't start until after he was dead. It was what he knew."

William turned sharply and pointed a finger in my direction. "Exactly, Father. And what I am saying is maybe, just maybe, Frankie knew too much. Maybe it got him killed!"

"You mean," said Andy, "he blackmailed the wrong husband."

William shrugged. "Maybe it's bigger than that."

"What could be bigger than that around Chandelar, unless it …" He stopped abruptly.

"Yes?" said William.

"Clear!" said Andy. "The Dew Line. Huge radar, lots of government stuff. I mean, the guy said he was from Clear. What if he really was?"

"It would make a lot of sense," I said. "He was driving a U.S. Army car."

"Maybe," said William, "Frankie found out something he wasn't supposed to, about something at Clear."

"A government secret," breathed Evie. "I read my Graham Greene. Government secrets can definitely get you killed."

"Spies?" said Andy. "In Chandelar?"

"It is a radar system," said William, "a line of defenses stretching across Canada and Alaska and Greenland, for only one purpose."

"Missiles from the Soviets," said Evie.

"There were spies at Pearl Harbor," said William. "Had been for years. It's probably safe to say that any government installation of significance, anywhere in the world, has spies."

"Naaaah," said Andy. "A spy would stand out like a sore thumb in Chandelar. It would be the shortest spy career on record." He laughed, but I didn't. Somehow, what William was saying was finally starting to make sense of the tangled web that had been Frankie's life—and death.

"So you think," I said to William, "that there could be Russian spies at work here—in Chandelar and at Clear?"

"Oh," said William, ducking his head to take a sip of coffee, "A government installation of this size and importance, I'm certain of it."

CHAPTER 16

The bullet shattered my shaving mirror, spraying bits of silvered glass. The point was clear, right between the eyes of my bewildered reflection. A thin rivulet of startlingly red blood oozed down my white, shaving-creamed chin. It was not a razor cut, but a small, triangle of glass lodged below my lower lip. I never heard the shot though others told me later that they did.

Ironically, while shaving, I'd been in the act of reviewing my progress with Frankie's list, deciding I was doing reasonably well, and feeling like a pretty clever guy. True, there was still the Masterson situation, but I guess I'd been doing a reasonably good job of talking that one down, at least to myself.

When my mirror exploded, I was too slow and stupefied to duck. It just never occurred to me that someone would be shooting in the middle of town. I stood there, trying to figure out what would make a mirror explode like that, until I felt an arctic blast of minus-thirty-degree air driving through the shot-out pane of window. A piece of burlap gunny sack, fetched from my pump room, stuffed the hole, and it wasn't until I'd swept up both the mirror and window glass that my knees started to seriously shake and I felt like throwing up.

It took a wad of gauze, held in place by adhesive tape, to stop the bleeding from my chin.

Minutes later, the quick knock, and Andy came in for his morning coffee. Seeing the wreck of my chin as he passed the door to my tiny bathroom, he said, "What's the other guy look like?" Then he saw the broken window, the burlap sack, and finally the bullet hole in what was left of my shaving mirror. "Holy shit," he said. "Let's close those curtains." That done, he grabbed a flashlight and hesitated a beat before heading out the door. Our eyes met. "I'm sure he's gone," he said. "That was just a warning shot or you'd be dead." But he went out cautiously just the same.

In about five minutes he was back, nodding to himself. "One shooter," he said. "Couldn't find the brass. No fresh tire tracks near ... looks like he walked."

The coffee helped, and we sat, clutching our mugs, trying to put puzzle pieces of my morning back together.

"You didn't hear the shot?" he said.

"No."

"Not at all?"

"If I didn't hear it," I said, "then it stands to reason I didn't hear it at all."

"Don't get touchy," he said. "I'm trying to help."

"I know ... sorry."

"It's okay. It's like that, being shot at." He thought a moment. "You know that's a helluva shot, a six inch shaving mirror from nearly a hundred feet. There's not many from around here could make that shot, and only one rifle." I gave him a look. "Hey," he said, throwing up his arms. "It wasn't me." Simultaneously, we climbed out of our chairs, grabbing for parkas and the keys to the truck, which had been

105

plugged in all night and started instantly. I had to admit it felt pretty good to have a pickup truck sitting in my driveway and not dead Frankie's.

Like most in the village, Andy kept all his firearms displayed on a rack in his living room. With the curtains open, as they were now, the rack was plainly visible from the street in front of the house. And like most Chandelar cabins, Andy's was seldom, if ever locked. It was possible he didn't even own a lock, just a hasp and padlock on the outside for when he was away.

The rifle was where it was supposed to be.

"Dead end," I said. But Andy grabbed it down from the rack and shot the bolt, sniffing the chamber. "Fired," he said. "Somebody hooked the rifle, shot at you, then returned it. Shit!"

"There goes the neighborhood," I said.

He laughed a little, but couldn't shake the worry lines from between his eyes.

"This Frankie thing is way out of hand. I'm not sure who you pissed off, or how, but this is definitely fucked! And I don't think it's Russian spies." He turned suddenly. "It's something you got from Frankie's. Maybe that list, isn't it? The one you found my name on." He gave me another of his sharp looks. "This isn't the first thing, is it—this shooting. Something else has happened. What? Tell me."

So I did tell him, about having the house tossed, about someone following me to the Mission, and one thing led to another, and soon I was also telling him about my midnight prowl of Frankie's place, and about not finding the will that the marshal easily found the next day.

106

"Shit," said Andy. And again, "Shit! You won't show me the list, will you? No? I didn't think so. Had to ask."

"But the people on the list, the ones I've talked to—they're off the hook! No more payments, ever. Unless they keep on doing the things they've been doing, and get caught on their own. But that has nothing to do with me. There's certainly no reason to shoot me in the shaving mirror."

"So it's something else," said Andy.

"What do you mean?"

"It's something in Frankie's stuff that you've missed."

I guess I had been thinking something similar, but not wanting to come to that conclusion. With Frankie on ice, it had been easy to think that a bad guy got what he deserved, however regretful, and that life would go on. But having another murder wasn't anything like having life go on, especially if it were my murder.

"Got your key?" asked Andy. "Let's go shake the place. Be like Sam Spade."

"Yeah, got it. I don't dare leave it around." We started out the door and up the path, and then I stopped. "Tell me something."

He stopped but didn't turn, like he knew what the question would be. "You went looking for the key so you could get your rifle back, right?"

"Yeah. And I knew about the photos—the Moses girl, and some of the other stuff. I knew it would all be in there somewhere, although I didn't stop to think about the safe. I didn't get a chance, of course. You got the key. And then somebody tried to torch the place. I was all for letting it burn, and it looked like you were, too."

"Yeah," I said. "For a few minutes, it looked like problem solved."

"Well, look on the bright side. At least you got a truck out of it … finally. Now that's a motive!" he said, and laughed. "I'd a killed Frankie if I thought I'd a got to keep the truck." And he laughed again. No one ever enjoyed his humor as much as he did.

We didn't need the key. Somebody with an axe had taken the lock and hasp completely out of the frame. The door stood wide open, with a fan of blown snow extending about four feet into darkness.

I was feeling around for the light switch when Andy grabbed my arm. "Hold!" he nearly shouted. "Don't touch that switch!"

"Damn!" I said. "Don't do that. I nearly jumped out of my boots. What is it?"

"Gasoline," he said. "I think I smell gas. Maybe nothing, but when the Germans cleared out of Italy, they booby-trapped everything. Coupla times we found wires hanging down from ceiling lights into cans of gasoline. You flip the switch and the whole place goes up in your face. Course they destroyed all the power plants, too. One more reason they lost the war. We've got to get a look in here," he said. "Got a match?"

"A match?" I said. "Are you crazy?"

"I jokes," he said. "I'm gonna move the truck around so the lights shine in the door. Stay put."

A minute or two of sliding the truck around in the drifted snow showed us what we needed to know. It was a length of lamp cord suspended into a red metal can of gasoline.

"Nearly got us," said Andy.

The place was a shambles. Books and girlie magazines all over the floor, boxes of business papers emptied and strewn, dishes broken, mattress gutted. Only the big Wilkes & Bodie Frontier Safe stood inviolate, though scratched and gouged, as though saying, 'This safe laughs at axes.'

Andy yanked down the wire, a cutoff length of extension cord, and capped the gas can. "Okay." He gestured at the switch and I turned on the lights. Then he didn't say anything, just stood for a long moment, looking thoughtful.

"What?" I asked him.

"Likely," he said, "whoever did this knew it would be you that came in and flipped the switch. You or …"

"Or Evie," I said.

"Yeah, or Evie." He thought some more. I let him. Finally he said, "I been hoping all this stuff, snuffing Frankie, shooting out your mirror, was some stranger sneakin' in, maybe a Commie. They're always warning us about them on the radio."

"Now?"

"Now I'm pretty darn sure it's somebody I told about the light-switch gasoline trick. Someone from around here. You expect this kind of thing from foreigners or Nazis, not from your own." He gave a visible shudder. "Gives me the crawlies." He pointed to the safe. "You got the combo?"

"Yeah." I did still remember it.

"Then open it," said Andy.

I might have opened it from memory, but looking down, spied the old bible and picked it up. "This guy would have had it too, if he'd spent more time reading and less time chopping." That's when the man with the mask stepped through the door.

"Open it, Padre," he growled. I might have laughed, except for the service .45 he had pointed at me. It was clearly the man calling himself Masterson. He was still wearing his military issue overcoat and his rubber galoshes with the snaps. Still wearing the silly hat with the earflaps, although accessorizing with the .45 made it all seem less silly.

Andy shifted suddenly, and Masterson turned and fired the .45. The shock wave of sound in the small space, clapped hard—painfully—like hands on both my ears. Startled, Andy flung his hands up as the slug furrowed the floor between his feet.

With Masterson distracted, I opened the Bible, took a quick step while cocking, and stuck the barrel of the pearl-handled Derringer under his chin. "Gun down, now!" I said.

He put it down, alright. He tossed it hard to the floor, where it fired. Andy, behind me, let out a shriek and hit the floor, while the recoil spun the pistol and slid it out of sight under Frankie's bed. In the same motion, Masterson twisted, chopping at my miniature weapon with the hard edge of his hand. Reflexively clenching, I pulled the trigger. With a staccato crack, the .32 fired one round into the ceiling, again rattling my eardrums. Masterson spun, all arms and legs scrabbling for the open door, wreathes of gun smoke, shifting and ribboning in the wake of his flight. Before I could do anything to stop him he was out the door, the snowy crunch of his footfalls, fading into the distance and the ringing of my ears.

Quickly I stepped to Andy where he lay, and knelt at his side. With no blood, no visible entry point, I began trying to find the wound by touch, just as I'd done so many times in France.

"Oh God," I said, an involuntary prayer for all the souls I'd seen slip away as I tried desperately to not let them—Mary—all the nameless soldiers in France. They formed a line of pure loss, stretching off in time and distance, and a re-opening of an old wound I was not sure I could continue to survive.

I could feel his body quivering, then convulsing—then he began laughing out loud as he pushed me aside and sat up.

"I jokes," he said. "Ticklish." Right about then I could have shot him myself.

CHAPTER 17

"It was supposed to be a diversion," Andy said, crawling under Frankie's bed to retrieve the .45. "No dust," came his voice, a bit muffled by bedding. "There's not a bit of dust under here. Weird." Climbing out, he trained the .45 on the doorway, while I shut and barred the door with the steel axle rod Frankie kept for that purpose. It was clear Frankie hadn't been taking any chances and now, neither were we. I worked the combination on the Wilkes & Bodie and together, we swung the massive steel doors wide.

"So that was Masterson," said Andy.

"Stands out," I said.

"Tell me what he said."

"I told you. He claimed to be a government agent from Clear. Wanted everything I had on Franklin Delano Nicolai."

"A government agent," said Andy, "from a radar site that's not even started up yet? Does that make sense? If William's right, Masterson could really be a spy, but could a real spy possibly be that clumsy? And we still don't have any idea what a real spy would want with Frankie."

"Not Frankie," I said, "Franklin Delano Nicolai."

"Wow," said Andy. "Been a long time since I heard anybody call Frankie by that name. Probably third grade."

"You knew Frankie since third grade?"

"Oh yeah. Frankie and Jerry and me were all in the third grade together at the Mission school. Frankie used to pay Jerry to beat up kids and take what they had—which wasn't much—a marble maybe, or a bottle cap. It wasn't so much he wanted the stuff as he liked being in charge and having power. One time, he told Jerry to beat up a kid who had a new harmonica. I told Jerry not to. Jerry wasn't too happy and Frankie got so mad he shook his fist at me and cried. Swore he'd get even." Andy looked away, a stare that took him far beyond the corner of the room. "Guess he got even. It took him awhile," said Andy. "He got my rifle." He raised his fist at the room. "Fuck you, Frankie!" he shouted, then ducked his head. "Sorry, Father," he said, and grinned sheepishly.

We turned to the open safe. "It's in here," I said. "It's got to be."

"But where?" said Andy, surveying maybe fifty cubbies, neatly stuffed with rubber-banded clumps of envelopes and paper. "And what? What are we looking for?"

"No idea," I said.

He grabbed the ledger, clearly marked 'loans.'

"It won't be in there," I said. "That's gonna be the part of the business that's legal. Well, most legal."

"Yeah, I guess," said Andy, swinging open the cover of the large leather-bound ledger. "Hard to believe there's so much business for a guy like Frankie to do in a little whistle stop like Chandelar. "Wow!"

"What?" I said, crowding around to see what he'd seen. "What did you find?"

"Nothing really," said Andy, running a weather-roughened finger across the page. "Just surprised to see so much stuff. So much business making people miserable. Just surprises me, that's all."

Together we pulled out and examined every bundle of papers, in every compartment in the safe. It was Frankie's usual assortment of nastiness. We were only two or three bundles in when Andy looked up at me. "We should burn this stuff," he said. So we did, gradually warming the tight little cabin with love letters gone astray, late-night desperate gambling IOUs—Frankie even owned a half-share of a Chinese woman, once some kind of physician in China and now a prostitute, in Talkeetna.

"Welcome to the good old U.S. of A," said Andy with a bitter laugh. "Save that out. I've gotta go down there next week. Be a pleasure to let her know her debt's been cancelled."

"This is only a half-share," I cautioned. "There's a partner."

"Bring him on," said Andy. "I'll explain to him how America is supposed to work."

One compartment held nothing but a photograph, an old one, of a young Athabascan girl at the Mission School. Andy saw me looking and reached over with finger and thumb to angle it his way for a look. "Know her?" he said.

"Evie," I said. I had seen its twin on my visit to the mission.

"Want me to give that to her?" he asked.

"I think I'll keep it," I said, and put it in my parka pocket. Andy smiled.

"You know what you're doin', right?" he said. He shifted into his version of an edgy character, like a carnival barker, who spoke out of the side of his mouth. "You come up here, all lonely. Wouldn't be the first cheechako to think life could be pretty sweet with a little Indian gal. But then, in a few days, or a few weeks—maybe more—you realize you can never take her anywhere else. Up here, she's the person you love. Everywhere else, she's Indian. Some places, you can't even take her to the lunch counter."

He wouldn't look at me, but wouldn't shut up, either. "Dark face like that, high cheekbones. You'd never get that big parish in Tennessee or New York, or anywhere, even if she has read every book in the god damn library and learned to talk in town."

He finally turned to look at me, his usually cheerful, open face, closed and twisted and bitter.

"You finished?" I asked him.

"Yeah," he said, "I guess."

"What was all that about?" I asked, but he ignored me to read something he'd discovered."

"I'll be dipped," said Andy, abruptly changing the subject. "A contract." He held it out.

"For what?" I took the paper.

"Murder. A year, two years ago, fellow from Minto took up with a waitress at Moocher's Bar in Nenana. Girl Frankie had his eye on. Couple weeks later, hunting season, this guy, Isaiah Charley, catches a bullet in his teeth. Coroner says hunting accident. But no." He held the paper up toward the light bulb, squinting at it. "A quick five hundred bucks to some shooter for his trouble. No name on this contract. Wish I knew who."

"He had him killed?"

"I told you, he liked the power." Andy stuffed the note in the stove. "That's it," he said, no clue here."

"Or we burned it," I said.

115

"Not the worst thing," said Andy. "Means nobody else is gonna find it either." He looked at me with a crooked grin. "What do you say we torch this place tonight? Finish up what somebody already started."

I just looked at him.

"Well?" he said. "Or not."

We closed and locked the safe and tied the door shut enough to keep small, wild critters out. If Masterson came back, he'd get through the door easy enough, but still have to deal with the safe. "Like to see him try," laughed Andy.

"Think Masterson is the shooter?" I asked, walking away. Andy considered.

"Nah," he said.

The sun had come up. Driving the short distance back to my cabin, we were half-blinded by sunlight reflected in a million diamonds off the snow. But our thoughts were still dark, back in the cabin, in the safe, in the search for Frankie's secret. The secret that had likely gotten him killed.

"What else you got," said Andy after a block-and-a-half of silence.

"Huh?"

"What else did you bring home from the cabin and hide?"

"What makes you think I've hidden something?"

Andy gave me an 'I'm being-patient' look. "Already know you've got the blackmail ledger at home. You showed it to me. And we pretty much tossed Frankie's place. Nothing there. Somebody else thinks you've got something hid, which is why they tossed your place, and ..."

116

"Okay. Okay. You're right. I did bring home a few things for safekeeping."

"Can we look?" asked Andy. "Are you gonna let me see what you've got? This isn't about keeping people's secrets anymore. Bet you I know most people's secrets around here, anyway, and I'm darn sure not tellin' 'em."

"So what's it about, then?"

Andy gave me a disgusted look. "You must have missed that class at the University. It's about keeping you alive."

Reluctantly, I showed him the ledger. Beside each name was a brief description. Next to the local principal's name, the notation: 'sex with secretary.' He quickly noticed, as I had, two marked-out entries, his and one other. With his fingertip planted to keep his place, Andy turned. "Need to tell you that …"

I held up my hand. "That your connection with Frankie is personal, and there's nothing about it that would get Frankie killed, or interest a government agent."

Andy let out his breath. "Right," he said. "Yeah." I could tell he was relieved.

"I knew that," I said.

There was a long moment of silence as Andy slid his finger down the column, his lips silently shaping the names and the offenses. "Thanks," he said, handing the ledger back.

I showed him the pictures, too. He flipped through them without comment or pause, except briefly over the first of the 'Roberta' sequence. "Worried about this kid," he said, and went on. There was reason to worry. Of maybe a hundred photos of naked women, Roberta was the only one smiling. Some looked

117

worried or fearful, some looked drugged, some were crying. Only Roberta looked like she was having a good time.

Andy looked at the front and back of each piece of photographic paper. Somehow he seemed not to look at the images themselves. Most men will look at a naked woman, just because she's there. I marveled at his focus, and felt uncomfortable that I had actually looked at the women.

"Not here," he said finally. "Nothing."

"We know he had something," I said. "Someone killed him for it."

CHAPTER 18

Roberta sat on the hard wooden chair across from my desk and didn't look at me. She was fifteen, dimpled, slim, pretty—though a bit sulky now—with brown eyes and shiny black hair worn in a long, thick braid extending nearly to her waist. The braid did a little up and down dance like a charmer's snake when she said 'yes,' and whipped back and forth like something even more menacing when the answer was 'no.'

It was whipping now. "Frankie never did nothing to me." She looked deeply into my eyes and smiled sincerely. The smile seemed nearly predatory.

"Nothing?"

"No." There was more braid whipping.

"Uh," I said, trying to be delicate, "your father said something about pictures." Something shifted behind her eyes.

"He said you'd been photographed naked. Uh … nude."

"No pictures," she said, so emphatically the braid ended up over one shoulder.

I decided to give up delicacy. "Can I tell you something?"

Again the deep-eyed, meaningful smile. "Sure," she said.

"I've seen the photos. I have them. And you are definitely nude."

I hadn't realized she'd been moving and twitching in the chair until she suddenly stopped and nothing moved. She didn't even look like she was breathing.

She dropped her gaze. "So whaddaya want from me?" She looked up. "More pictures?" She smiled again. "We could work somethin' out."

Her offer caught me off-guard and I found myself stammering. "N-nothing. I don't want anything. Except, I do have a question."

She didn't say 'sure' this time. She was much more cautious with cards on the table.

"What's the question, and what's it worth to you?"

"The truth," I said, "that's what it's worth to me. I want to know if you killed Frankie? But before you answer, you need to know that there isn't a jury in the land that would convict you for it. They'd probably line up to shake your hand."

She stared at me.

"So you don't have to be afraid."

"I'm not afraid," she said. "I never been afraid."

"So it doesn't seem like there's any reason why you can't answer my question."

"Except maybe I don't wanna answer your question. Maybe I don't wanna play your game. Maybe I don't like you."

"I don't get it," I said. "Or maybe you don't get it. You're off the hook. You don't owe anything to Frankie, your Dad doesn't. That part of your life is behind you now. Aren't you glad?"

"Glad?" she said. "Frankie was a clown. He was a fool. But he'd do anything I asked him. He'd take me anywhere—he took me to Fairbanks just to buy me a pair of shoes. He gave me money. He just about bowed and prayed to me, especially when I was taking my clothes off. The first time he saw my boobies, drool ran out the corner of his mouth. I'm not kiddin'." She leaned across the desk, and jabbed the leather blotter with one finger on each syllable. "*Ev-ry-thing-I-asked*," she said. "We was gonna be married in July when I'm sixteen, but for somebody pinched him off like a candle flame. Now I got nothin'."

She looked me over like I was on the menu, nearly licking her lips. "But you and me can have some fun," she said, and ripped the front of her red-checked flannel shirt completely open, spraying buttons across the floor and exposing what looked like an expensive silk bra.

"Make me an offer," she said.

"What?" She had lost me.

"Tell me how you're gonna make my life better, and tell me quick." She was ramping up to something. Abruptly she was nearly shouting, face reddening. She pulled the ribbon off the bottom of her braid and threw it on the floor, and flipped the braid back and forth as she spoke, messing it with both hands as she became increasingly disheveled. And then she stopped and turned to me.

"I go out the door screaming," she said, "and you're done. No more church. No more priest. Jail— I'm only fifteen you know. There's probably a beating in it for you, too." She stood abruptly, upsetting the chair, already overbalanced with her heavy parka, and kicking it. She pulled her shirt clear back off one shoulder, gave it a rip for good measure, and smiled at me. "What's it gonna be?" she said.

I admit I was dumbfounded. "Nothing." I said. "It would be … wrong."

She smiled at me, a sad, pitying smile. "You're a loser, too." She stared out the window and smiled. "The public health nurse just walked past," she said. "She'll make a great witness." Roberta started to scream and run, and I was already imagining the court, facing the bishop, and probably jail time, when Evie stepped up to lean on the office doorframe. She'd come in the front door, during the tantrum, without either of us hearing her.

The scream choked off like a little soprano hiccup.

"What kind of witness will I make?" asked Evie, very softly.

Roberta swayed, like she might topple. At the last second, she threw herself against Evie, wrapping her arms tightly around Evie's neck and holding on hard.

"Oh god," she sobbed. "You're just in time. He ripped my clothes. He touched me. You know what I mean. You saved me."

Evie pushed her off. "Cut it out. How long will it take you to learn not everybody is as stupid as Frankie?"

"No," cried Roberta, "you have to believe me."

"I don't have to believe you. Smart doctors and priests have nurses and assistants as witnesses, because of people like you." Evie turned to me. "I believe you wanted an answer about Frankie."

I stood up, weary—suddenly so weary I wobbled. "I got it," I said. "She answered the question. To think," I said, "I was feeling sorry for her because of Frankie. Now I'm feeling sorry for Frankie. Probably the first time in Frankie's whole miserable life anybody felt sorry for him. She wouldn't shoot him. She thought Frankie was her golden goose. Somebody else turned him into a dead duck."

CHAPTER 19

I live in one of the few cabins in town with running water. This luxury is courtesy of an aging piston pump in the lean-to addition at the back. The room has its own small heater and is heavily insulated to keep it from freezing solid. The water heater is there also, and it is not unusual during the long winter months, to have people from the town stop by occasionally and ask if they might trade something for a hot bath in a bathtub.

On Friday nights, when people come by to sit in my living room, drink endless cups of coffee and talk, there is also a good deal of washing and flushing that happens. It is all part of the tapestry of village life. It's frequently an all-male gathering: Andy and Jerry, William, and Steve who smokes a pipe and runs the town's electrical generator. But sometimes the public health nurse stops by, or the town's postmistress, and as it happened on this particular night, both of them, and Evie.

She knocked and entered, as has become her custom, then stopped somewhat shyly at the sight of my living room filled with all these people. There was a heartbeat of surprise in the room, and probably calculation—she came in the door very quickly and comfortably—and then it all started up again, with requests that she would stay awhile, join the talk, and have a cup of coffee. With a little coaxing, she did.

We talked about Al Kaline, my favorite topic, then drifted to probable statehood—not a popular topic. President Eisenhower was good by this group, but nobody thought Vice President Nixon had much future, to which I had to agree—although they did like his wife, Pat. A lynching in the South kept us busy for a while, with general agreement that the United States was a racist nation, and had always been so. And then Evie told us, to my great surprise, about the three months she lived in New York City, attended NYU, and was generally thought to be Puerto Rican and treated very badly.

I talked about Tennessee, the little town—Sewanee—where I had gone to seminary. It's a little mountain town, off the beaten track. Even though there is a colored section in the movie theater, and "colored only" drinking fountains, I remarked that it had been a congenial place and that people had seemed to get along pretty well.

Since more than half the room was Athabascan, this wasn't well received. Andy talked about the lack of racism in Italy, and William talked about the war—frozen bodies stacked like cordwood—and Evie said that "separate but equal" was always "separate but unequal," and the very fact that everyone is not treated the same means that they do not have the freedom the Constitution guarantees. The room was silent when she finished, and then we all clapped. She was eloquent. She blushed and rose with her coffee cup in a little bow, and the spell was broken, the evening at an end.

I admit I hated to see her go, but I knew she had to. It would be social suicide to stay behind as everyone else was leaving. A thing like that would be an item on Tundra Times, a Bush gossip show on Fairbanks radio, by tomorrow afternoon. But I had come to enjoy our unexpected meetings, and moments of talk about nothing in particular. My campaign to get all the local people, at least on Frankie's list, praying for her recovery, kept her constantly in my thoughts.

So after the crowd filed out, I was washing coffee mugs in the kitchen when she rapped and quickly entered. "Let me help," she said, grabbing a dishtowel and aggressively polishing my collection of chipped and stained mugs, which certainly didn't deserve the attention she lavished upon them.

"That was fun tonight," she said. "It seems I don't get to be around people much, and especially people talking about real things. I mean everybody talks about the weather, or getting a moose, or going to the States or something."

"But not ideas," I said. "Thoughtful stuff."

"Yeah," she said.

Dishes finished, we drifted in comfortable silence back to the living room sofa and settled with backs at either end, facing each other. She had kicked off her boots and was sitting, knees up, chin on knees.

"So how are you?" I asked.

"Fine," she said. "Fine."

"No," I said, "I mean how *are* you?"

"Um," she said, "actually—this is probably my imagination—but I think this lump is a bit smaller. It seems smaller and less hot. Can that happen?"

"Have you heard of remission?" I asked her. She hadn't, and we talked about that possibility for a bit.

"I don't want to lose you," I said. I hadn't meant to say it, I just opened my mouth and suddenly there were the words hanging in the air.

She raised her eyes to mine for an instant, then dropped them. "I don't want to be lost," she said, "but …"

"But what?"

She looked up blinking, because her eyes had begun to tear. "I would only say this to you as my priest, and my … friend. I believe I have this—this cancer—because I deserve to die. Because God wants me to die."

The notion left me speechless and the silence was a roar in the room. "How can you even think that?" I asked, finally.

"Because," she said, "I haven't lived a particularly good life. I've deliberately done things I knew I shouldn't. Haven't done things I knew I should. I think you've heard enough and seen enough to know that I'm not a saint. And I appreciate that you've been fair and even with me, even knowing what you probably know, even thinking the things about me that a person, especially a priest, couldn't help but think. That's all." She laughed a little, embarrassed, and wiped her eyes on a sleeve.

"Let's clear up some of this," I said. "I'll tell you exactly what I think about you, and then you only have to worry about real things and not vague fears. First, I think you're a good person …"

"No, not good," she said. "Not good."

"A good person, a kind person, who's made the best of a bunch of bad situations. God gave you brains, and you're using them. That's what you're supposed to do. Everybody makes mistakes. God forgives them. There's no interest owing, no penalties. Nobody is keeping score. At least that's the way I see it. The key line is, 'Go now and sin no more.' If you can't live with your old life, change it. Don't sentence yourself to death, especially a death like this one. Live. Do good work. Make yourself happy. That's what God wants for you. That's what I want for you."

She didn't say anything, just sat, snuffling, hands covering her face. "I don't know if I can believe all that stuff," she said.

"Why not," I asked.

"Because the bad stuff is easier to believe, and I started believing those things at a younger time in my life, when the things you believe sneak inside who you are and stake their claims." She got up suddenly, hands still over her face, stumbling on her boots where she'd kicked them. "Gotta go," she said, and quickly pulled on her boots, grabbed her parka and hustled out the door, closing it firmly behind her.

The moment or two after Mary had gone and they turned off the iron lung, I realized that I'd never been in such a completely empty room. It felt like a yawning chasm of emptiness, that I knew in my heart could never be filled. I'd lost some of that empty feeling during these last months, moving to Alaska, starting at the Mission, making a few friends. The room had begun to fill, I'd thought. Until now. At this moment, the room was back to full empty and I was suspended out in the middle of it and starting to sink. I didn't know if I could bear to go all the way to the bottom again.

And then she was back. I heard the door open, her footsteps through the front room, her shape in the door, her quick steps to where I sat. She leaned down quickly, tipping my head back, and kissed me briefly but firmly on the lips. Then she left again, and I could hear her footsteps crunching away in the snow, and taste the salt of her tears on my lips.

But the kiss caught me, reeling me back in, and the room seemed less empty and deep.

CHAPTER 20

"Subtract line eleven from line thirteen," I read from the instructions, and that's when the phone rang. I had been helping old Mr. Levi Silas with his Federal income tax form for 1952. He was running a bit behind.

I picked up the heavy black receiver. "Father Hardy," I said. At first no one spoke. I heard commotion—someone shouting something about a gun. I had already started a personal adrenaline storm when heavy breathing—panting—came on the line, then an Athabascan voice. He shouted something.

"What?" I shouted back, startling Mr. Silas, who slowly rose to his feet, watching, listening.

The voice shouted again then hung up suddenly. "What?" I shouted again, too late, and looked at Mr. Silas, probably a little frantically.

"What did he say?" he asked mildly.

"I don't know. I heard shouts—something about a gun—I'm afraid it's something serious, but I don't know what. It didn't make any sense. I couldn't make it out."

He smiled calmly. "What did it sound like?" he asked.

I shook my head in frustration. "It sounded like he said 'caribou on ice.'" We stood staring at each other for a long moment, then shouted in unison "Caribou on ice!" Mr. Silas ran out the door, still zipping his parka, while I grabbed my ancient 30-30—my father's Kentucky deer rifle—stuffed myself into my parka, grabbed the truck keys, and went out the door on the run.

It took a few minutes to unplug the truck's heater, start the truck and let it warm up enough to be able to get it into gear and moving. Even so, I overtook Mr. Silas, still about a block from his cabin. He jumped to the running board before I could slide to a complete stop. "Go, go," he shouted, pounding on the truck roof, and I did. At his cabin, it took him less than a minute to grab some ammo and his rifle, an old World War I 30-06, and we were once again on our way to the river.

We found them at the Standard Oil dock by the Tanana. Andy was there, and Jerry of course. As I stepped from the truck with Mr. Silas, William came puffing up to join the group, carrying his rifle in a custom case with flaps and snaps. Andy seemed to be in charge. Right now he was dividing the group into mushers and shooters, some rushing off to hitch up teams, some loading and fussing with guns.

I looked at Andy. "Where?" He pointed down the river. I don't know if I'd seen them if he hadn't pointed. A quarter mile or more away, a caribou herd of maybe twenty animals was cantering out of an ice fog across the river ice. Somebody handed me binoculars. I made out twelve bucks. Clouds of their warm, moist breath caught the sun and turned to gold in streams. When one of them took a nervous look back, I followed his gaze. That's when I saw the wolf pack.

"Wolves," I said. "That's why they're running."

"No way," breathed Andy, and grabbed the binoculars. "Meat and wolf bounty! Looks like this is going to be a good day," he said. "Finally."

"Cheez," said Jerry. "I get first shot," he called, then looked at Andy. Andy looked back. "Use the big gun?" asked Jerry. Andy nodded and handed him the sniper rifle.

Jerry took it, sort of caressed it, wrapped the sling around his arm, and assumed his shooting stance. I saw him slowly breathe in, out, in—the rifle cracked—and the big bull in the lead shuddered, but kept moving. "Nuts," said Jerry, and made to hand the rifle back to Andy. Andy held up a palm.

"You, Father," he said. I looked at my 30-30.

"Too far for the deer rifle," I said.

"Think so?" said Andy, and held out his hand for the rifle.

"Use this one," said Jerry. "You're not gonna make that shot, and we can't afford to …"

Andy had grabbed the carbine, levered a shell into the chamber, turned smoothly while bringing the gun to his shoulder and squeezed the trigger. It was a clean headshot with no scope, and the wounded buck sank like a stone.

Andy looked at Jerry. "It's not the gun," he said. There was just a heartbeat of hesitation, and I would swear I saw something pass between the two, something old and dark. Then, Jerry grinned his goofy grin and Andy turned away.

"Mine," shouted William. We all turned to watch. I'd never seen a gun like his. It clipped into a single-pole stand for front support. It had a long scope, maybe twice the length of Andy's. "Watch closely boys and girls," said William. Which is when I looked over my shoulder to find that Evie and several other of the women had arrived. I looked back in time to see William casually squeeze off a single shot that dropped

132

the next big bull. Andy was spotting. "Nice shooting," he said. "The old guy gets the prize."

"Old guy," William huffed. But I could see he was pleased with himself.

In all, we took four of the bucks, and didn't have to wait long for teams to be harnessed and back to the river, each to pick up a shooter and set off in pursuit. They would kill as many wolves as possible, a notion that was only popular because the Territory of Alaska was paying a bounty for wolf ears, and there weren't that many ways to get cash around here.

Andy handed back the carbine. "Nothing wrong with the rifle," he said.

"Except the shooter?" I said.

"Shooter needs practice," he said, and clapped me on the back, encouragingly. He turned. "William," he called, "where'd you get that Roosky gun?"

William laughed a crafty laugh. "Stole it off a dead Russian," he said.

"You guys always shoot your caribou from the Standard Oil dock?" I asked Andy.

"Hardly ever. We don't get caribou around here that often," he said. "Been … ten years." He turned to Jerry. "Take any caribou out here while I was gone?"

"Nah," said Jerry. "Not since before the war."

"You going out?" Andy asked me. "Looks like we're walking …"

"Let's take the truck," I said, watching his face light up.

"Take the truck!" he said. "That's a lot better than hauling meat back here by dogsled for the next twelve hours. Truck's a great idea."

The truck bed quickly filled with villagers with rifles, long knives, butcher's aprons and meat saws.

Since the highway to Nenana ran out on the river ice anyway, all we had to do was follow the wind-cleared patches in the direction of the meat. The one drift we hung up in, the crowd jumped out to push and we were quickly on our way. With so many hands to help, and the 'Frankie memorial truck,' we were back in Chandelar with the first big meat of the season, in less than two hours.

We stacked caribou parts to the top of the wall. Tomorrow Andy, Jerry, and the meat saw would divvy up the kill to the other townspeople. And just in time. There were a lot of empty meat sheds around town.

It was dark when we finished, Andy making the last cut with the meat saw by candlelight. "You're eatin' at my place tonight," he said. "Don't tell me you got no appetite. Maybe we can get Evie to come over, too. You ain't tasted caribou roast 'til you tasted my caribou roast."

He was right.

CHAPTER 21

I woke during the night again—or dreamed I woke during the night—when came tiptoeing into my bedroom. Moonlight washed the room silvery blue and backlit her so I could see the enticing outline of tipped-up nipples through her cotton nightie.

"Aren't you cold?" I asked, my words a silver cloud. In better days, I might have followed with, "Hey baby, crawl under these covers and I'll warm you up."

Hooo, I've heard that one before, she said, seeming to read my thoughts. She perched on the footboard, looking thoughtful.

You're going to have to kiss her, she said.

"I don't want to kiss her."

Actually you do, or you would, if you weren't busy being faithful to me. And that's the problem, she said.

"Why is that the problem?"

She gave me a patient look. *You're being faithful to a dead woman. It's no way to live.*

"I like seeing you like this," I said, hoping to shift the topic.

Yeah, it's nice, she said. *I hated that iron lung.* She held her hands out like Tinkerbelle. *Now I can flit about.* She gave me that 'I'm going to be trouble' look. *So you still like the nipples,* she said.

"You can read my thoughts!" I said, with a certain amount of dread.

I never had to be dead to read your thoughts, Hardy, she said, and rose. *You were always an open book.*

"I love you," I said.

I know you do, and I know you always will. But listen to me now. Your heart is like a big gunny sack and the more love and joy you put in it, the more it opens up to hold.

She gave me a long look. *And eat,* she said. *You're down nearly eighteen pounds. You look like a rack of bones.*

"Not eighteen," I said.

Yes, eighteen. That's why you had to poke that new hole in your belt.

"Anything else," I asked her, sensing we were out of time.

Just a question, she said, moving toward the door and already growing gauzy. *What was Frankie's body doing so far from town? That's what I want to know.*

"That's what I want to know, too," said a strange voice. But suddenly it was morning. Mary and the moonlight were gone and that strange voice was mine, a lonely, sleepy voice mumbling from under a mound of blankets in a cold, empty room.

CHAPTER 22

Bob, bartender at the Borealis, called me just before midnight. "Guy here talkin' 'bout something to do with you. Can't make it out exactly, but could be trouble. Thought you'd want to know," he said guardedly. Would I come?

Trouble at the Borealis usually meant one of my soft-spoken, amiable, parishioners having too much to drink, shouting and picking fights. I would show up, collect my drunk and see him safely home, which would be far better than having him set off on his own, only to pass out in a snowdrift and likely freeze solid before morning.

"On my way," I said, as I padded back out of my study, in my woolly slippers, to the living room. Evie startled up on the sofa where she'd been stretched out, fast asleep.

"What time is it?" she demanded. Crooking her elbow, she ran her hand through her thick hair, then froze in that position, looking around dazed and trying to wake up.

"Bob at the Borealis," I told her. "I've got to go."

"Why did he …" she said. Then again, "Why did he …" But she couldn't seem to get to the end of the thought.

"… call you?" she said, finally. She took her hand out of her hair and stretched out an arm to squint

137

at her watch. "Near midnight," she said. "Why so late? Is it trouble?"

"Nah," I said, "piece o' cake." But I admit I was hearing Bob's voice again, trying to not make something of it. Something to do with me, what could that be? I thought of the snub-nosed .38 in my desk drawer. It's funny that if the gun weren't there, I wouldn't have thought of needing one. Maybe handguns create their own danger.

So I sat on a wooden kitchen chair and pulled on my mukluks. Evie sat up and reached for hers. She was wearing an olive sweater over a white blouse, and men's jeans, that somehow looked very fashionable on her.

She had showed up, late afternoon for coffee, and stayed to scramble eggs and sizzle a bit of canned bacon, while I made toast, spread with chips of real frozen butter. I still hadn't gotten on to the new margarine. I didn't mind the taste but hated having to mix-in the yellow color.

After dinner came more coffee and a slow, natural procession into the living room, talking, laughing, all the while. She had a graceful, flowing way of walking when she was relaxed, sort of straight legged, swaying each hip wide, and I was grateful to be following along behind.

We ended up dipping into my store of nearly three months of unread Life magazines, reading interesting bits to one another. Hemingway—Papa—the magazine called him, was still in Cuba. Here in the States, children were practicing 'duck and cover' drills in school, in case the Reds attacked, and college students were featured in an article about squatting. Squatting to read, talk, smoke, flirt, study. Apparently it was all the rage on campus to squat. Before reading the article it had seemed like a thousand years since I'd left the University—about eight months ago—and after reading the article, it seemed like two thousand years.

"Just going to rest my eyes," Evie had murmured as she stretched out on the sofa, and the next minute was snoring softly. And the evening passed like we were two, old married people, secure in ourselves and in each other. She rolled over on her side, facing the back of the sofa, and I admired the curve of her hip, and rose to cover her with a woolen blanket. I remembered evenings like this with Mary at Sewanee. A part of me had believed that I would never have one again. But here we were. And too soon, it was nearly midnight and the phone was ringing, and life was moving ahead and dragging us along.

"Don't go," she said. "Bob knows how to do this. He knows not to send them out alone."

"It didn't sound like that," I said.

"You mean like trouble?" she said. "He wouldn't call you for trouble. Besides, he has a sawed-off shotgun behind the bar, and he knows how to use it. Whatever it is, he can handle it."

I pulled on my parka. "He called me," I said. "Gotta go."

"Ohhhhh," she grumbled, but then standing, turned to smile. "I had fun," she said. "It seemed so ..."

"Companionable," I said, but I was thinking settled.

"Yeah, that's it." She pulled on her parka and smoothly flipped the hood up over her head. "C'mere you," she said, and threw her arms around me in a roughhousing embrace that was suddenly tender, kissing me on each cheek. Then she walked me out to the road, heading off home while I went to see about Bob.

This time of night, deep and dark and silent, the Borealis stood out as an oasis of color and light on the otherwise darkened and deeply snow-shouldered street. Neon signs for Olympia, the king of beers, and Budweiser, clicked on and off as I approached, flashing the piles of sidewalk snow unnatural shades of red and blue. Even out here in the street I could hear Pat Boone singing, "Ain't That a Shame," his new hit. But just as I reached for the door handle, I heard a terrific crash, and the needle shriek of the jukebox and then it all stopped, and I opened the door, stepping into a tense, silent room.

The Borealis was the big bar in town, with the room fifty or sixty feet long, done in smoky, yellowed knotty pine, with a low, white-squared, acoustic tile ceiling, a small dance floor of waxed, slippery hardwood—empty tonight—and a large, chromed Wurlitzer jukebox, bathed in its own blue-white glow at the far end. Coming in the door, the air was hard with the stale stench of old cigarettes, beer—pungent sawdust on the floor—and faint overtones of urine and Lysol.

Bob was behind the bar, hands out of sight. He was a smallish, intense Caucasian with glasses—metal-rimmed on the bottom, plastic on top—receding black hair and a fierce, hawk-like nose. There were maybe six or eight customers, spread out at tables around the room, drinking singly or in pairs. Moments ago, they may have been hunkered over their beers, now all eyes were on Bob and a tall stranger, weaving and nasty at the back, with the jukebox all ajar where he'd probably kicked it.

The man was big, well over six feet, and he stood up a bit taller as I entered, then sagged back into his drunken slouch when he satisfied himself that I wasn't something he had to worry about. He wore a dark, heavy woolen overcoat, and his head was bare with a close haircut that might have been military. "Another drink," he shouted at Bob, lurching toward the bar, spittle flying. From my vantage, at the side, I could see Bob flinch, almost imperceptibly—something he didn't usually do. Instead of answering, pouring the beer, or exposing the shotgun, he turned to me, coolly putting a smile on his face.

"Evening Father," he said, "the usual?"

"Sure," I said, even though we both knew I didn't have a 'usual.' Bob popped the cap on a sweaty Oly and had it up on the bar and slid my way before the big drunk could snag it. I caught it, flipped my hood back and dropped my mitts, and took a drink of the cold beer. It tasted good, surprising me. Since Andy didn't drink, and I wasn't likely to drink alone, I had let the notion of beers this cool and refreshing slip away.

"Thanks Bob," I said, wishing I'd brought the .38.

"Father gets a beer and I don't?" said the big drunk. He turned to face me. "Father of what?" he said, and started for me. "Ohhhhh," he said, "Father …" as if realizing something. "You're not my father," he said, and started in my direction. That's when the shotgun came out behind him. Bob's eyes met mine and I shook my head. Slowly he made as if to replace it on the shelf behind the bar, but from where I was standing, it looked like he kept it in his hand.

"You want to give me the beer or get a beating?" he bellowed.

"You're drunk," I said. "Why don't you head on home and sleep it off."

Instead of answering, he swung, with a long left that came in so high and slow it might have filed a flight plan. I'd dodged hotter punches than this in grade school, so it was easy to tip and turn my head as the fist went by, at the same time, stepping aside to be out of the way of his scarcely-controlled fall when he didn't connect and overbalanced himself.

But he managed to catch a grip on the bar, and push himself back upright, then advance with two, ham-like fists clutched up under his chin.

"Hold your beer, Father?" asked a familiar voice. I turned my head slightly. It was Andy. Evie had made straight for his place instead of heading home. They must have jogged back.

"Long as you save some for me," I said, handing off the stubby with my left hand while tipping my head out of the way of a serious right jab. It looked as big and slow as a freight engine, chugging past my right eye. Shrugging out of my parka, tossing it on a chair, I held up my hands in a gesture of 'let's talk this over.'

"Don't hurt him, Hardy." It was Evie's voice.

"Hurt him?" I don't think the top of my head even came to his chin. "Couldn't we talk this over," I said to him.

The big guy faked a right cross then aimed a leather work boot at my groin. I wasn't able to get completely out of the way and the force of the blow caught my upper thigh and spun me half around. He let go a right-left-right combination too far back to do damage, but then stepping in, rattled me a bit with a knuckle slam to the side of my head.

Out of the corner of my eye I saw Andy move from one table to another. I wondered if this was some kind of rescue scheme he was putting together. He seemed to be urging a man in a red felt hat to do something. Another rap to the side of my head brought me back into the fight and convinced the red-hat man to do whatever it was that Andy was asking.

I hadn't been in the ring for two years or more, but now something was happening. I was bobbing, weaving, shuffling. I could feel the first light sweat on my skin and I began to remember how much I had liked boxing. "Get up," Mary had said. It made me smile, which spooked the big guy and he let go with a mighty right cross—that missed.

Everything went into slow motion for me and it was like he'd sent that long, thick arm out there and parked it. I stepped in close with a short, quick left and then a right that caught him just above his belt buckle, buried itself in a surprisingly soft middle, and bent him over my arm. I stepped back, smelling his burst of sour beer breath, wanting to be out of the way of the vomit, if that happened.

As his head came back up, I put my whole shoulder behind a hard right to his chin that rocked him back against the bar and down into the sawdust on the floor. He took so long to get back on his feet that I had begun to think the fight was over. But then he came up, unfolding a knife with a very long blade, shaking his head and spitting a tooth and a clot of blood.

I jumped back as he lunged. Nothing connected but the barrel of Bob's shotgun alongside the big man's head, putting him down and out. Bob kicked the knife away from the stilled fingers. "Shouldn't have brought a knife to a gunfight," he said, and let out a little cackle. "Last call, boys," he said to the room. "Beers on Bob."

"Here you go, Father," said Andy. He handed me a hat full of cash.

"What's this?" I said.

"Money," said Andy. "Nearly four hundred dollars."

"You took up a collection?"

"Won it," he grinned.

"You were betting on the fight?"

"Absolutely." He laughed. "Put that in your old mission barrel!"

CHAPTER 23

"So this guy was asking about you?" said Andy. "That's why Bob called?"

"Who was I? Where did I live? Pretty unusual for a guy I never met."

"Bet he's wishing the two of you never met right now. Bob seriously whacked him with the sawed-off, and you punched out a couple of his teeth. Sure makes you wonder why a guy you never met, from someplace you probably never been, knows enough to ask questions about you."

"I was going to try to ask him about it when he woke up. But they dragged him outside for a few minutes, just for the cold air, went back to check and he was gone."

"That's pretty weird, too," said Andy. "Didn't look like he was going to be up much, moving around. He went down hard." We fell silent for a few moments, sipping coffee, thinking, and my mind snapped back—again—to Mary's question in my dream.

"What?" said Andy, sensing the shift.

"Something I've been wondering," I said. "What was Frankie's body doing so far from town?"

Andy looked up from stirring sugar and canned milk into his second cup of coffee, the spoon clinking. "Yeah," he said. "I've been wondering about that myself."

"Is there anything out there?" I asked. "A fish camp? A cabin? Something in summer?"

"Nothing really," said Andy, "especially in summer. Place we found Frankie is an island—well, a big sandbar—with a narrow slough on the backside. In summer, no way to get there without a boat. It's kinda off the beaten track. I hadn't been out there in years, but Jerry wanted to take a look, and why not. We weren't finding anything to shoot anywhere else. And there Frankie was, like you seen him—shot and froze. So," he took a sip and made a face. "Can't imagine what the slippery son-of-a-bitch was doing out there."

"Sorry, Father," we said in unison. Andy took another sip of coffee, grinned, and nodded at his coffee mug. "No offense," he said, "but this stuff is awful. Even milk and sugar don't hide the truth."

"Hey," I said. "This stuff comes out of the red can that means good taste." He made a wry face. "If you don't like it, don't drink it."

Andy feigned panic. "Got any more?" he said. "Gotta have it."

"I think we need to go back out there and look around," I said.

Andy made a face. "Out where we found Frankie?"

"I think we need to take another look."

"You're forgetting something," he said.

"The shaving mirror?"

"Yeah."

"I'm not forgetting." I fingered the scab on my chin. "I just don't think anybody is going to shoot us in the middle of the day, especially if we can sneak out of town."

"So that's your plan," he said, "sneak out of town?"

"I'm open to suggestions."

"Fresh out," he said. "Mind if I bring Jerry along? Strength in shooters."

"How much do we have to tell him?"

"He already knows somebody took a shot at you. Tell him it's bodyguard duty. He'll be thrilled."

"How does he know somebody shot at me?"

Andy rolled his eyes. "You're in Chandelar now. Everybody knows. Most knew before the echo faded. Go out today?" he said.

There was a knock at the door, a knock so tentative it was easy to imagine a small, chilly bird, hoping to come inside. "Uh-oh," I said.

"Trouble?" said Andy, setting his mug on the table, looking alert.

"Not that kind of trouble," I said. "I bet you nothing that this is Mrs. Neilson."

"Mrs. Big Scotty?" said Andy.

"Afraid so." I answered the door, and it was Mrs. Neilson. I assured her that, yes, I'd come right away.

I left Andy to finish his coffee. "Tomorrow," I said, going out.

He saluted me with his mug. "Tomorrow."

~

Big Scotty looked and smelled like he really might be dying this time. His large, unwashed body totally filled an old metal army cot stuffed up along one wall of the long, narrow tar paper shack that Mr. and Mrs. Big Scotty called home. A similar cot, neatly made up with a hand-sewn quilt lined the wall opposite.

147

"Would you please make us some tea," I asked Mrs. Big Scotty.

"Oh yes," she whispered, eyes on her mukluks. The whole place was dim, lit by two hanging, un-shaded, forty-watt light bulbs. Electricity had been an afterthought here. Plumbing, too. The kitchen sink drained into a bucket, concealed behind a flower-sack drape. The toilet, a five-gallon bucket with a white toilet seat on top, hid behind a curtain at the back.

Normally I would pull up one of the kitchen chairs, turn it around and straddle it for our talk. With the one-room cabin so tiny, the beds and the kitchen table stood nearly side by side. Norman Rockwell covers from old *Saturday Evening Posts* softened the walls, which were otherwise lined with cardboard and layers of newspaper for insulation.

"I'm dying, Father," said Big Scotty. There were tears in his eyes and the corked end of a whiskey bottle protruding from beneath his pillow.

Normally I would tell him that I didn't think he was dying, he was drunk, and we'd speculate on the nature of life and death, the price of beaver hides, and whatever else seemed significant, usually for much of the day. It would be a fairly pleasant day for the dying man and a long slow one for me. Today I had decided to try something different.

"This time I'm really dying," he said.

"I know," I replied. Big Scotty's eyes fluttered open.

"You know?" he said. "You know I'm dying?"

"Yes," I said, "I can see it. I'm sorry to lose you, but I understand that this is all part of God's plan—and yours—not mine to know about or to change." At this point, instead of sitting down with him,

148

I pulled a tape measure out of my parka pocket, along with a pencil and a small notepad.

"Hold this right here," I said. Placing the tape end at the top of his head, and waiting until his thick fingers caught hold, I stretched the tape to the bottoms of his feet. "Six foot two and three-quarters," I said to the room, and wrote the number on my pad.

"Six-four," said Big Scotty. "Umm, what are you doin'?"

"Measuring," I said.

Behind me in the room I heard Mrs. Big Scotty's breath sharply intake. I had to lean over Big Scotty to measure him, shoulder to shoulder, across his sizeable expanse. No job for a smoker. His breath and any kind of open flame would have been explosive.

"Measuring for what?" asked Big Scotty. He had begun to try to squirm himself into a sitting position. I stopped to write my next number. Mrs. Big Scotty had begun to weep and rummage in the cabin's only closet, emerging after a few moments with an old, flat, dusty cardboard box, tied with a string.

"Measuring for what?" said Big Scotty again, but by now he was sitting upright. "Well," I said, and that's when Mrs. Big Scotty appeared with the suit. Crying and sniffing, she gently pushed her husband back flat against the pillow and laid out the pants and the vest and jacket across the top of him. It was seersucker, white with thin blue stripes, circa sometime in the late thirties. Then she leaned a pair of two-tone brown-and-white wingtip shoes against the footboard of the bed, just on either side of the dying man's feet. The dying man, I now noticed, had begun to sweat.

"Looks like I'll have to let it out a little," she said to me, as though Big Scotty had already moved on.

149

I nodded gravely but she didn't move and stood staring at me. "Make the note," she said finally, and winked.

"How much does he weigh," I said to her.

"Two-sixty," she replied without hesitation. I wrote that, too.

"Two-forty," he said. He was sitting again, clumsily folding his suit.

"Is that for my ..." He couldn't seem to say the rest.

"We'll have to get Andy and Jerry to start building a fire," I muttered to myself. "Thaw the ground," and made a note. "Or," I said, "do you have a meat shed here?"

"Ground softer in spring," she said.

That's when Big Scotty sprang out of bed. I'd never seen a man his size move so quickly.

"You know," he said, swaying slightly, "I'm feeling a little better."

"Next of kin?" I said to her.

"Just me," she said. "I think."

"And a son in Ohio," he said.

"Really?" she said. "A son? Maybe I could go and find him. I've always wanted a son."

"I'm feeling a lot better now," said Big Scotty. Then he stopped, threw his arms up in the air and shouted. "It's a miracle! I'm *cured!*" he shouted, loudly enough that several mice startled from cover, sprinting back and forth across the narrow floor, each trying to find a hideout that wasn't already taken.

"Thank you Jesus!" I said.

"Amen," said Mrs. Big Scotty. She grabbed the whisky bottle out from under the pillow, pulled the cork with her teeth and went behind the curtain to pour the remains into the honey bucket. When she came out, she looked directly at me, smiled a sweet smile and started across the room to the wood-fired range.

"How do you take your tea, Father?"

CHAPTER 24

All the teachers—seven of them—lived in stateside-like apartments, in a three story, wooden building called the teacherage, across the street from the school. Unlike most of the rest of the village, the teachers had plenty of electric lights with wall switches, hot and cold running water, electric refrigerators and ranges, a laundry, and central heating from a coal furnace at the back. Among the town's one-and-two-room log cabins and tar paper shacks, this slightly shabby clapboard structure seemed somehow grand here, like baronial mansions I'd seen in England or France.

About once a month, the teachers would get together for a potluck and party. I was routinely invited, as an educated person and—I suspect—a single person. Two of the teachers were unmarried women. Sometimes the public health nurse and her husband were there, and sometimes the storekeeper and his wife, or one of the CAA couples from the airfield. They all came in sets except me, and of course all of us were white.

On those nights, everyone would drink a bit too much. Pipe and cigarette smoke would wreathe ruddy faces in the lamplight as stories were told of the south forty-eight, of people and lives left behind for the move to the last frontier. Most of them felt very happy and alive to be in Alaska, like they were living life on the edge, which they were, and doing something that mattered, which was also true.

As part of their transition to frontier life, most of the men were bearded. Some wore hunting knives on their belts and one or two was wearing rubber-bottomed, knee-high, leather boots laced outside their trousers. Women were wearing brightly patterned flannel shirts or sweaters with things like poodles stitched on. They wore tailored women's khaki or denim trousers, zipped at the side, with a stylish vee at the ankle, generally revealing a tantalizing glimpse of waffled long underwear. Most of the women were wearing something on their heads. There seemed to be several ways to wear a scarf stylishly, which they did, and one wore a beret.

But in the midst of all this gaiety, it was pretty clear that the unmarried women were lonely. In a territory where men outnumbered women dramatically, they were alone. If any of them had gone to where the available men actually were—a bar—their tenure as Alaskan schoolteachers would have been over. They reminded me of expatriots in France, after the war. Drinking too much, smoking too much, and keeping to themselves too much. So, by the end of an evening, I'd find myself centered on a sofa between two lonely, desperate women who would have gone home with a grizzly bear if he'd clean up and make small talk.

One of them—Francine—was pale, shapely, dark-haired and brown-eyed with full lips, highlighted by the latest stateside shade of vivid red lipstick. She alone wore a dress, dark green with buttons up the front, and sheer nylon stockings, something none of us had seen for a very long time. It was as if she had the only ankles in the room and it was hard to not watch them as she moved about. She hadn't come with bare ankles, it was forty below outside; I suspected she'd simply bunched her long johns above her knees. She was desperate to dance and, as if in answer to her prayers, I heard an album drop on the Philco, and the honeyed voice of Nat King Cole, singing "Stardust," began to mellow the room.

"Father?" She said the word with difficulty.

"Yes."

"Do I have to call you Father?"

"No," I said, but nothing more. I knew I was being ungracious, and knew that something about the situation was making me feel awkward.

"Would you like to dance with me?" she said.

The answer was no, I wouldn't like to dance with her. But I knew she was lonely and bored. It would be nearly suicide for her to dance a slow dance with any of the married men in the room, even though it was likely that some of them would be all for it. Francine wasn't at all hard to look at.

"Sure," I said, and stood up, took a step or two forward and assumed the dance position. We started fine. Her right hand was raised in my left, with nothing touching between us but flannel. But by the chorus she had dropped my hand, put both arms around my neck and cinched us up tight, with her thigh somehow moving, not at all timidly, between mine.

"Francine," I said, and then was unsure what to say. Ease up, was all I could think of. So I said it. I felt eyes of the other teachers on us, and knew this dance would get us top spot on the hit parade of weekly gossip.

"If you'll walk me home."

"You just live on the other side of the building."

"We'll take the long way."

It seemed safe enough. What could happen walking around a building at forty below? "I'll walk you home if you'll leave ten minutes before I do and wait by the Jensen's cache."

"Deal," she said, and gradually widened the space between us, though leaving her arms around my neck. "When?" she whispered, under the final chord.

I smiled, as though she had said something funny. "Not too quickly." I said. These people weren't stupid.

She smiled back, as though I had said something funny. "Okay," she said. As the dance ended, she patted my arm lightly and made her way carefully across to the refreshments table, where I saw her select a palm full of peanuts and a shallow glass cup of the high-octane spiked punch. It was what they liked to serve on these occasions, and then all watch and see who had too much and said or did something stupid. They weren't mean people. On the contrary, they were good people, but it was midwinter and they had Alaska-sized cases of near-fatal boredom.

Francine tossed a peanut into her mouth, took a sip of her punch, shook her head, as if to clear it, and eased back to her single friend on the couch. I began to breathe again as I felt eyes leave her and conversations around the room rekindle.

About twenty minutes later, in the middle of a conversation about outboard motors, I felt a shift in the room's energy and heard Francine's voice. "Night everybody," she called out. The women gathered for pats and hugs and air kisses on the cheeks while the men stood across the room in a semi-circle, waving and smiling. Next to me, the science teacher waved, smiled—made sure his wife couldn't hear him—and said softly, "I'd like to be following that one home."

"In your dreams," said another.

"Got that right," said a third, drawing on his straight-stemmed pipe. I didn't say anything, but then I already had a date to follow that one.

"So the prop fell off," I said, and for the next ten minutes our hearts and minds returned to last summer's balky Evinrude.

True to her word, Francine waited on the road edge by the Jensen's cache, in the moon shadow of a huge mound of plowed snow. She was stamping her thin-soled, stylish, stateside boots in a vain, impatient attempt to keep her feet warm.

"Do you have any idea how blinking cold it is out here?" she blurted, then softened. "I was afraid maybe you'd changed your mind." Her words were clouds of moist breath silvered by the light of a full moon, so bright it cast dark, distinct shadows on the snow.

"Sorry," I said. "I had to wait."

"I know," she said, "it's okay." She turned. "Let's go this way."

I hesitated, pointing back toward the teacherage. "You live that way."

Now she hesitated. "Not all the time," she said. "C'mon."

In the distance one dog barked, then another. More distantly, a dog—or a wolf—began a long, resonant, tremulous howl. *One of God's loneliest sounds,* I thought.

"Here," she said. We turned off the bladed road onto a sled-width trail, boot-printed in about six inches of snow. "I'm living back here," she said, "sometimes."

I followed in her boot prints. Out here alone in the night, it seemed an intimate act. "I didn't even know there was a place back here."

"Most people don't," she said over her shoulder.

"How did you …?"

"A friend," she said.

At the cabin, she pulled off her right mitt, revealing a knit glove, supple enough to allow her to retrieve a key from her parka pocket. The key fit a silver padlock on a hasp. She turned the key but then had to yank open the frozen lock. She pushed the door open, stepped in, and motioned me to follow. It was already warm inside.

She had the key, so it seemed likely this was her place, but I was troubled by the feeling that we were sneaking, and wasn't sure why.

An electric light came on, a single bare bulb hanging from the ceiling by a twisted cord, activated by a turn switch. She'd been here often enough to find it in the center of the room in the pitch dark.

"Your place?" I asked.

"Well," she said, "it's a long story. Want a drink?" When I hesitated she added, "Or coffee?"

"Nothing, thanks," I said.

"Oh c'mon, a cup of tea then. Have a cup of tea with me!"

"Okay, a cup of tea."

The cabin was one square room, with a kitchen, dining table, and double bed occupying three corners, and a blanketed-off fourth corner that was likely a closet with a honey bucket. She poured water from a gallon jug into a kettle, turned the knob on a small, old-fashioned propane range, the color of putty, and struck a wooden kitchen match to light the burner. Then she shook out the match with her right hand, while pulling off her left glove by tugging the middle finger with her teeth.

Shrugging herself out of her parka, she said, "I guess I came on pretty strong back there. I'm sorry."

"It's okay," I said.

"I …" she hesitated, then turned, talking with her back to me. "I just really wanted to have the chance to sit down with you and …" she hesitated some more. "… and talk."

"Oh," I said, and began to imagine that, in spite of the very personal come-on, this was really priest business.

"It's just that I heard about what you were doing. I mean, I know that your wife died and that you're up here all alone, and I know how lonely it can be, up here all alone.

"It's not so bad," I said, still to the back of her.

"Well, you have to say that," she said, "but I know you have your needs, and that you …" She stopped. "… that you're still a man and …"

I interrupted. "What are we talking about?"

"The prostitute," she said with difficulty. "I know you're seeing a prostitute. For sex," she blurted. "And I know," she said earnestly, "I can save you from that. I want to."

I sat down suddenly. "Francine," I said. And that's when she turned to face me. She had unbuttoned her dress and now shoved her waffled long johns smoothly over her thighs to the floor. Straightening, she was naked up her front, save for boots, a garter belt and stockings.

Okay, it wasn't a priest thing.

158

"Francine," I said again. She spread her arms and would have run to embrace me, but for the long johns bunched around her boots at her ankles. So she sort of shuffle-hopped, but the result was the same. She pulled my face tightly between her shapely breasts and patted my back soothingly.

The smooth skin and warmth was nice against my face, and I could smell her hair and her perfume. I might have wanted to stay in that position a long moment, even if she didn't have my head in a near death grip.

"Francine?" My voice was muffled against her body. "What are you talking about?" Her grip loosened a little, but it was the whistling teakettle that saved me. It started softly but quickly became too shrill to ignore. So she let me go and shuffled off to pour boiling water over our teabags.

While the tea steeped, she kicked off her boots and stepped out of the long johns. Most people are better looking in their clothes. She actually looked pretty good naked. She smiled when she saw me looking at her, and I must have blushed. "No," she said, "I'm glad you're looking at me. I want you to look at me. I want you to make love to me, not that prostitute."

"Francine, I'm not ..." She held up a hand.

"You don't have to deny it. And you don't have to be ashamed of your needs. I know all about your problem."

"You know about my problem?" I echoed. She nodded.

"And I'm here for you," she said.

"How do you know about my problem? And what prostitute?"

"My … friend," she said, "told me you were so desperate that you were paying for sex. He told me he saw her coming out of your cabin, early one morning."

"Saw who," I said, but suddenly I knew where this was going.

"The prostitute. Evangeline Williams."

"What friend? Who would tell you something like this?"

"I can't tell you. It's private."

"It can't be more private than you telling me that I'm paying for sex because I'm needy."

"Well, that's different. You can't help that."

"Who told you all this, Francine?"

"Well, I … I've met a man," she said. "I know you'll probably say that I'm being impetuous, or that we're too different. But he's got some money coming, quite a bit, actually, if he can just manage to get his … employer to pay him what he's owed." Her eyes softened and her voice took on a dreamy quality as she began to describe the life she and this soon-to-be-wealthy man were planning. A small house in Sausalito, with a picket fence, garden space and an easy walk to the shore. "Of course I hate to leave here midyear … break my teaching contract, but …"

"Francine, who?"

"It's Jerry," she said. "Jerry Charlie. He's got plans and dreams—ambitions. He's the one renting this place for me. Don't be upset. I know he's your friend. He's the one who told me everything."

CHAPTER 25

We went out from town about five a.m., nearly five hours before sunrise, under a hard black sky, pierced with a million dagger-points of silver stars. A small breeze turned the already bitter cold painful, and I had a scarf covering my face almost to my eyes. I was wearing my high, canvas, military-surplus mukluks and a long, military parka reaching almost to my knees. I decided to not bring the deer rifle, but at the last minute, slipped Teddy Moses' snub-nosed .38 out of my desk drawer and into my parka pocket. You never know.

I had awakened and dressed in the frigid chill without lights, without even turning on the furnace. I slipped out the back door slowly, soundlessly easing closed the usually squeaky door. Somehow I managed to make it away without setting off the sled dogs tied next door. Though they all had straw-lined doghouses, they seemed to prefer sleeping curled up in small, dog-shaped donuts in the snow. Sometimes, after a night of falling or drifting snow, they disappeared completely, until one stood up, startled, barking. Startling one would be startling all, but for now, they slept on.

Several minutes' walk on a shallow path through my small woods brought me to the street behind, to Andy, with Jerry—rifle ready—standing off about forty feet, watchfully.

"You made it," said Andy softly. "Good." He handed me a pair of long, leather-laced snowshoes, strung with a shoulder strap for packing, then turned with a quick step and headed off up the snow-packed road, leaving me to fall in behind. He was carrying a similar pair, tied to a small backpack, with the sniper rifle slung from his shoulder. Jerry fell in at a distance behind us, in case of ambush, I supposed.

The ambush by Francine, the previous evening, had never really left my mind. Awake or asleep, I had pondered it through the night, coming to no conclusion, except that there was more going on in Jerry's life than I'd known. The idea of Jerry and Francine as a couple frankly astounded me. I had never known a more dissimilar pair. With difficulty I turned my thoughts to the project at hand.

In a few minutes we reached the dogsled trail that would lead us out on the river ice—locals still called it the "mail trail"—and within about fifteen minutes we were out of sight and sound of the still-sleeping town.

Starlight, reflected off the snow, gave us a distinct gray outline of trail to follow. Beyond, a dark fringe of willows revealed the rise of riverbank. Any other time, being out on the trail with these two, in the predawn stillness of this wild place, would have seemed like an adventure, like a gift. Not today. The only sounds: the wisp of frigid parka fabric, and the slight, squeaky crunch of snow under our mukluks. Only sled width, the trail wouldn't allow two abreast. I closed distance with Andy. "You really think we're in danger?" I asked. It was hard not to whisper.

"Don't know what to think," he said softly, over his shoulder. "In Italy, I was hunting men and they were

162

hunting me. Everybody understood the rules. But I wasn't expecting that here. Course, whoever shot your mirror could just as easily have put that bullet in your ear—which tells us something. Not sure what."

We walked in silence for a time. Andy was right. But somehow, not being shot was more likely a function of the shooter not having found what he was looking for. Once he had the goods, whatever 'the goods' turned out to be, I wondered what would keep him from putting a bullet in one of us—most likely me.

"Oh crap," said Andy.

"What?"

He motioned Jerry closer, pointing. Out of the gloom cantered a bull moose, intersecting the sled trail. He was tall, with a broad rack, and would have been just right for hauling back to the meat shed. Jerry looked at the moose, then at Andy. "Nuts," he said. "If you shoot him here, we're not sneakin' anymore."

"Yeah," said Andy, reluctantly. The caribou harvest on the river had eased the food situation for the moment, but it wasn't enough meat to last the winter. "Maybe we can pick up his trail on the way back."

Jerry laughed a humorless laugh and, as soon as the moose—an animal known to be short sighted—had crossed unknowing in front of us, we started off again.

About an hour out, Andy circled us up and handed us each a speckled metal mug. Producing a Thermos from his pack, he poured still-steaming, sweetened coffee into each. The coffee, luke-cool after having been poured into frozen cups, was nevertheless refreshing, fortifying—even oddly tasty—with a cold, dry baking powder biscuit to gnaw.

"This is still Frankie's fault," muttered Jerry between sips, and the two laughed. "Didn't get a moose the time we got Frankie, didn't get one now trying to get back to where he was. His fault." They laughed again. It was easy to imagine them as children on the playground at the Mission school, laughing together. It was also easy to imagine Andy calling the shots then, just as he did now. It occurred to me to wonder what Jerry's life had been like with Andy away in the war.

We soon reached the spot where our previous sled tracks cut off the main trail, as we came out to haul frozen Frankie home. I spotted the scrap of red flannel, gray now in darkness, still hanging as a signpost.

"What are we lookin' for," asked Andy, not for the first time.

"I don't know," I said. "Some notion of why he came out here. Why he died all the way out here."

"So we'd have to haul his stiff ass home," said Jerry, who laughed his goofy laugh, then looked somewhat sharply at Andy, who hadn't.

"Smoke," said Andy. Tipping his head back, he sniffed again.

"That's crazy," said Jerry. "Nobody out here. Must be blowing out from town."

"That's crazy," said Andy. "We're nearly five miles out." He pulled his rifle off his shoulder and slipped the bolt to chamber a shell. Jerry looked at him for a long moment then did the same.

"You're not doin' that bad dream war stuff again, are you? Who you expectin' to shoot out here?"

"Somebody shot Frankie," said Andy, "right here. Don't want to be next, do you?"

"Heck no," said Jerry.

Andy looked at me. "Stay behind me," he said. "Jerry, go wide, but keep us in sight. Make sure you don't get out in front of us."

164

"Check," said Jerry. He crouched to buckle on his snowshoes, then angled out on our right. Even with the snowshoes, the going was rough. Stumbling along through deep drifts, he was still at the mercy of buried branches and tripped more than once, holding his rifle up out of the snow, even as he slipped to his knees.

"Snowshoes," said Andy. We had them on and buckled in a minute or two. Snowshoeing wasn't my specialty anyway, and I had to pay careful attention to not step on the backs of Andy's snowshoes, which would pitch him on his face in deep snow, a serious predicament when your feet were still at the top of the snow, buckled into your snowshoes.

Jerry hadn't gotten ahead of us much, maybe fifteen feet, owing to the deep snowdrifts and the willow shoots. With the wind in our faces, the scent of smoke grew stronger. "What's a cabin doin' out here," muttered Andy. "It's a damn sandbar! Under water half the time." And on we went.

Just as we saw a flicker of window light ahead, there came a near-deafening explosion, close on our right. A bullet splintered a three-inch willow just above our heads, propelling us into a low crouch, both of us looking for something to duck from or shoot back at.

"Jesus Christ," said Andy in an explosive whisper, and then, "Jerry, you okay?"

"Yeah, okay," came a muffled voice. "Shit." He'd tripped, fallen hard, and discharged his rifle on the way. Lodged in a snowdrift, completely out of sight, he now rose, shaking, spitting and brushing snow from his face, his neck, his parka hood, and cursing—eloquently for Jerry—nearly under his breath.

The light went out.

"That's not good," said Andy. "If he wasn't hiding, he'd a come out and called to us. 'Come in for breakfast or coffee or something.' Don't feel right."

Ahead of us, near where the light had been, came a raucous sound, echoing and unexpected: an engine starting. "Chainsaw?" I said.

"Iron dog," said Andy, disgustedly, rising from his crouch. "Snowmobile. They're outta here. You okay," he asked, as Jerry came stumbling up to us in the deep snow."

"Yeah, okay," muttered Jerry. "Feel stupid? Cheez! You bet."

"Shit happens," said Andy, but I saw the look on his face that Jerry missed. It was one I hadn't seen before, and not a happy one. "Let's get a look at this place."

Moving in, we spread out a bit, with rifles ready. "Nothing supposed to be out here," said Andy again. "There's water here come summer. Has to be a boat."

Turned out he was right. What we reached, in the first early glow of dawn, was a boat, now adrift on a sea of snow.

"Taku Star," said Andy. "Washed out last breakup in the flood. Thought she was a goner, smashed in the ice."

The Taku Star turned out to be a small sternwheeler, just a mostly-covered cargo hold with a pilothouse at the bow. The pilothouse windows had been plywooded with what looked like that expensive three-quarter-inch government plywood from the Clear dump. There was still glass in the door, which was how we'd been able to see the light.

166

"Hello, the Star," called Andy, when we stood about twenty feet out. There was no answer. Only smoke from the chimney that rose, then chilled and fell back to creep along the ground, simulating life. "Cover, Jerry," said Andy, as the two of us moved forward, easing up a rough gangway of willow poles to the narrow side deck. A brittle breeze raised a small rattle of snow pellets against the wooden hull as we stood listening. "Feels empty," said Andy, after a few more minutes standing. "Jerry, circle. See what you see."

Jerry actually loped off around the stern, on snowshoes. I couldn't help but admire his ease and grace, the rifle held across his body about waist high. "He's good," I said.

"Yeah," said Andy. "Most of the time."

Moments later Jerry came chugging around the bow. "Clear," he called out, still in a low voice. "Snowmobile, all right. Gone now. Looks like they warmed it with hot rocks off the stove." He stopped, training his rifle barrel forward a bit.

To Andy he said, "Father opens the door, you and I cover?"

"Sure," said Andy. Then softly to me he said, "Don't get in front of that door. Work the latch with this." He handed me a leather bootlace with a loop end and then shifted himself down the deck a few feet to better back me. "Hear me?" he said.

"Yeah." My back to the cabin wall, I slid along the deck to the dark-metal door latch. Pulling off my bulky mitt, I exposed only my hand in its dark, olive drab woolen glove. I slipped the loop over the latch, eased back a step or two, and pulled.

The door exploded outward with a roar and a shower of glass and pulverized wood. Anybody

167

standing in front of the glass would be bleeding out now, not having any notion of a double-barreled shotgun, booby-trap rigged with a strong piece of cord through a screw eye to the inside handle of the latch.

Without warning my knees buckled, and I slid down the cabin wall to sit on the icy deck. For a brief instant, I thought I might even throw up. Andy hustled past me, sweeping the cabin interior with a small flashlight. "Gone," he said, "but not forgotten." He patted my shoulder. "You okay, Hardy?"

"Not shot," I said, "but not okay." I felt like the war had started up all over again, with me in the middle. And I had absolutely no idea who were the bad guys.

CHAPTER 26

"Where does this go?" I asked, pointing. The trail, a neat sled-width cut, steep sided by three-and-four-foot drifts, curved off through a willow thicket into the shifting gray of dawn.

Andy dug up his parka sleeve for his Timex, glanced at the position of the soon-to-be-rising sun, and worked his brain for a long moment. "Probably Clear," he said, "maybe ten, fifteen miles that way. Fits with the Sno-Cat, too. Nobody in Chandelar has one. Only one or two in Nenana. Gotta be Clear," he said again. "Maybe government guys. They could afford one, but what would government guys be doing out here— shootin' people?"

From inside the pilothouse came Jerry's voice. "Nothin' much in here."

We filed in. The double-barreled shotgun had been tied and braced to a pair of wooden chairs, nailed to the floor. It had been installed so securely that even firing both barrels at once hadn't moved it.

"Looks like they knew we were coming," said Andy.

"Huh?" I said.

He pointed. "Door on either side but they knew which one to aim the shotgun at." He looked around. "Not much here. Looks like they musta been camping."

He was right, there wasn't much: a pair of narrow bunks at the back, two chairs bracing the shotgun, and a small wooden table. The spoked ship's wheel was still in place, as were brass levers, gadgets, and even one of the old speaking tubes, for communicating with the engine room.

Andy gave Jerry a hard look. "Where's the photo?" he said.

"What photo?" said Jerry.

"The one I saw on the table when I first looked in here. Naked white woman."

"Tossed it in the stove," said Jerry, grinning his 'Jerry' grin, but with eyes suddenly hard and cheeks reddening.

"Like heck," said Andy. "Give."

"Aww, can't a guy have some fun," he asked. "Just 'cause you don't look at sex stuff doesn't mean the rest of us can't." Sheepishly, resentfully, Jerry unzipped the top of his parka and dug for what turned out to be a picture of a naked, middle-aged, probably drugged white women, propped into a pose on what looked a lot like Frankie's bed. Jerry was wrong. There was nothing sexy about the shot. It was obscene. "Bingo." I said.

"Connects," said Andy.

Jerry looked from one of us to the other. "What's goin' on here," he said.

I opened my mouth, but Andy said. "Don't know. Somethin' to do with Frankie. Found a bunch of pictures like this when we went through Frankie's safe." We both saw something flicker in Jerry's eyes.

"More pictures?" he said. "Can I see 'em?"

"Burned 'em," said Andy. "Too many familiar faces. Too much trouble if they get around—any more than they have. Looks like Frankie was trying to get some big porno action going—make a few extra bucks."

Jerry's laugh had a hollow sound. "Frankie was a dumbshit," he said. "Taking all them pictures in town. Think it was a husband that shot him?" He laughed again then looked at us looking at him.

"What?" he said.

"You've seen the pictures?" asked Andy.

"Well ... I've seen a few. Mostly just heard about 'em, you know ... around."

There was something about the tone of their conversation that made me nervous, nervous enough to drop off my mitts and sink my gloved hands deep in parka pockets. "Cold hands," I muttered, but I doubt that either heard me.

"I never heard that Frankie really sold those pictures," Andy was saying.

"Oh yeah, he did. I mean, I heard he did."

"Well, from who—who told you? Who has 'em that we could look at?"

"You said you already seen 'em. That little Roberta—hubba hubba!" He grinned but it wasn't working.

"We better get back," said Andy, cutting him off. "This whole thing feels wrong. Now we're out here, these other guys could be headed for town with plenty of time to get into whatever they want with no bother from us." He turned to me. "They knew we were coming." He headed out the narrow door, sideways along the rail and easily jumped the three or four feet into the drifted snow. I was right behind him with Jerry somewhere back of me.

"What I'd like to know ..." said Andy.

171

That's when the men in white suits erupted from the snow, almost at our feet, and one of them jabbed the muzzle of a service .45 at Andy's temple.

"I'll take it from here," he said to someone behind me. I turned to see who it could be.

"Cheez!" said Jerry. "What kept you?"

"We were just listening. It's important to know what we are up against. Not much, it seems. Get back to town and clean up those details we discussed. Hear?"

"Yeah, I hear," said Jerry. "Andy here was just talkin' about that." He stepped up and slugged Andy in the face, hard, rocking him back a step but not down. "I'll take this," he said, grabbing the sniper rifle.

"Leave it," said the man. "It must be found with the body. It might be all they have to make the identification." Regretfully Jerry let the rifle fall back into the snow.

"Waited a long time for that one, didn't you," mumbled Andy, spitting blood.

"Should have been a bullet," grunted Jerry from a crouch, rebuckling his snowshoes. He laughed, clearly excited at the way the day had turned. In fact, he seemed nearly euphoric. "Guess you're not in charge now, are you," he said, "not the big guy—the war hero. Funny, you went all the way over there, shot a bunch of people—got your shiny metal—and then you had to come all the way back here to die in the snow by the Tanana. Just sorry I can't be here to pull the trigger. But when the trigger is pulled, think of me." He laughed again, nodded at the two in white suits, and then snowshoed away, rifle across his shoulder, headed back to town and to whatever mischief he had left to make.

"Remember what I said," called out the one with the gun. "It must look like an accident." The other one set about with a small can of gasoline, dousing the boat.

"Got it," said Jerry over his shoulder. "I know what I'm doin'." They watched until he dropped out of sight down the river bank and off on the ice trail toward town.

"You're gonna kill us," said Andy.

"Yes, as soon us you give us some information."

"If you're gonna kill us anyway, why should we tell you?"

"Because it will make the difference between going into the fire before or after you're dead. I think 'after' probably feels a lot better, don't you?" His tone was so light and easy, he might have been talking about whether or not to go to a basketball game, not whether to burn to death a couple of guys he couldn't possibly have a personal grudge against. "So, what will it be?" he asked.

"I suppose," I said, "that there's no way to talk you out of this?" Andy gave me a sudden, odd look, as though picking up a vibration in the chill air.

"There is no chance at all," said the man I'd come to think of as Mr. Glib.

So I shot him, right through my parka pocket, three times. The holes lined up neatly on the front of his white parka, the red bleeding through as he staggered, trying to raise his gun arm. Then knowing he wouldn't, he pitched forward on his face in the snow.

A sudden whoosh of fire coincided with my pistol shots. A smaller but not less significant blaze— my parka on fire from the muzzle blasts—kept me from attending to the other would-be killer. It's not a scene I would forget: Mr. Glib pitching forward, Andy scrabbling in the snow for his rifle, grabbing it, rolling to fire; the other man in white jumping down from the burning boat, rifle up, sighting, trigger finger squeezing, then the sharp rifle crack—but it wasn't his rifle.

From behind me, someone had fired another shot into his eye, exiting the back of his parka hood in a spray that stained red the exposed, frosty hull of the burning boat.

I admit I thought Jerry had returned to save us, in spite of the wicked punch he'd laid on Andy. But it wasn't Jerry. It was another man in a white, arctic suit, masked. Only his peculiar rifle gave him away.

"William!" I said. "What are you doing here?"

CHAPTER 27

"William?" said Andy from his seat in the snow. He carefully lowered his rifle into his lap. "William, it's you?"

"It is me alright," said William. "You are correct." Leaning his rifle against a willow, he used both hands to pull off the white knit mask that covered his entire face.

"What is that thing?" I asked.

"In my country, it is called balaclava," he said. "I participated in snow training before the war, in Norway." He pointed to the two dead men. "Them, too. That is where the polar uniform comes from. We were soldiers on skis. Skiing and shooting at targets. It was quite fun then, but not so much, later. How did you recognize me? Oh—the rifle—from the caribou hunt."

"Yep."

He nudged the shoulder of one of the downed men with a mukluk toe. "Notice the outline of a patch there?" he pointed. "East German."

"There was no East Germany before the war," I said.

He grinned and blotted his drippy nose on his parka sleeve. "You are correct."

The three of us stood, nobody saying anything. *What were East Germans doing here now?* I wondered.

"Father," said Andy, nodding in the direction of the dead men.

He was right, and it bothered me that I had to be reminded to do my job. With holy oil unavailable, I made the sign of the cross on their foreheads with clean snow, giving last rites, though it seemed pretty clear that their souls had already departed this life, thanks in part to me.

As if sensing the drift of my thoughts, Andy said, "It was him or us. You gave him the plain chance to change his mind—that's when I knew you had the gun. He pointed. Recognize this guy?" It took a minute but I did recognize him: the drunk from the Borealis bar fight.

"No more bar fights for him," I said. "Thanks to me, no more anything."

"Let it go, Hardy," said Andy, the second time I noticed him calling me by name. "This guy didn't give the right answer, so you did the only thing you could do. You saved our lives."

"I must commend your most excellent shooting, by the way," said William. "How did you do that?"

"Pointed it like my finger and pulled the trigger," I said. Truth was, I was as surprised as they were. I never did that well in my Army sidearm training.

"What happens now?" asked Andy. He twitched his rifle, nearly imperceptibly in William's direction. There was something in his voice that betrayed the idea that we might not be out of trouble. "We need to know what you're doing out here," he said to William. "Grateful and all for having our lives saved, but it's still a fair question. Five miles from town, very early in the morning in your white army suit." He stared directly into William's eyes. "Time to tell," he said.

176

"It is no secret these fellows were up to no good," said William. "I had known you found Frankie out here, and had heard about your shaving mirror, Father. Of course I wanted to help if I could. As it happens, I was following a buck moose, a couple of miles back, and getting ready for my shot, when these two fellows came skiing out of the gloom, being very careful to stay off the trail. One of them skied right into my crosshairs. I let them go by, started back after my moose, and that is when I saw you three. I put it all together, picked up their trail and managed to get close enough to do you some good. That is the whole thing," he said, meeting Andy's hard look with a direct gaze and a friendly smile. "If I might make a suggestion," he said, "that we head back to town, as quickly as possible. You heard Jerry and his accomplice. This is not over."

"You're right," said Andy. I saw him begin to relax. "What are we going to do with these two?"

"You know," said William, "it wouldn't be the worst idea to throw them on the fire. It might smooth things out along the way."

I considered. Andy considered. It had become a big fire, raising a plume of first white and then black smoke as flames found the diesel left in the fuel tank.

"No," we said, nearly in unison.

"Be easy to do this one little thing," Andy said, "burn these bad guys. Heck, they meant to burn us. But then we're slipping out onto thin ice, having to move very carefully, probably in way over our heads, hiding things, covering our tracks, and one day asking ourselves if we're really doing the right thing. Or not asking, which isn't better."

"William's steely gray eyes locked to mine, then flicked to the man I shot. "You are right," he said. "You

177

start down a trail for all the best reasons, one thing leads to another—one day you look up and you have gone too far, with no way back—if you see."

I did see. With a sudden start I realized that he seemed to know, or have guessed, a great deal about what I'd been up to lately. So much that I couldn't tell whether he was talking about him or about me.

So we turned the two face down and left them to freeze in the snow. Andy said he'd get someone to come out and help him bring them in. I said that it would be me. We both knew it wouldn't be Jerry.

"I want to look at something," said Andy, and left William and me by the burning boat to follow Jerry's track along the trail toward the river.

William nodded at Andy's back. "A good man."

"The best."

"So you trust him," said William.

"Absolutely."

"You make trusting sound so easy."

"Takes about the same energy as not trusting," I said, "and feels better.

"What if he had some weakness, something you didn't know about? Something that someone else might use as leverage against you?" I shrugged, not knowing exactly what he was talking about.

"What I'm saying," I said, "is that I consider Andy to be my friend."

"A friend?" said William, as though amazed at the concept. "Well, what about Jerry? Did you trust him like you trust Andy? Was he your friend? Is that why he was along?"

"He was along because Andy brought him. I suppose if I did trust him, it was because Andy did, although …"

"Although you are thinking that Andy may have had … reservations."

"Something like that," I said, ending our conversation as Andy headed back our way, jogging.

"Better get moving," he said, quickly pulling on his pack and grabbing his snowshoes and rifle.

"What were you doing?" I asked.

"Looking for Jerry's tracks. I wanted to make sure he left when he said he did. Would be just like Jerry to hunker down and keep an eye on his buddies. He doesn't trust anyone."

"If Jerry gets to town before us," said William, "there will be no one who can keep him from hurting whoever he has to, to get what he wants."

Andy nodded.

"At least he doesn't know we're still alive," I said.

"Probably not. But he's got a pretty good lead on us. Being alive is an advantage, maybe our only advantage. Not sure it'll be enough. "

CHAPTER 28

"The part I don't get," I said to Andy's back as we walked, "is how Jerry was so stupid as to hang around and flunky for Frankie all these years?"

"Stupid?" he said. "Don't even think it. Jerry's one of the smartest guys I know. For one thing, he's always listening, not talking. And he's always got an angle. So I guess I'm not surprised he's tied up in this. He's wanted to punch me for years. Funny though, these guys thinkin' he works for them. My guess is it turns out the other way."

"Think that's what happened with Frankie?" I asked.

Andy shrugged. "Boy, I dunno. You thinkin' Jerry shot Frankie? I'm not sure he would. He's an altar boy, you know. Raised that way. Body and blood of Christ. Not that he wouldn't shoot a stranger if he wanted. Just not someone from the mission. He might of got someone else to shoot Frankie. Guess that wouldn't surprise me. He's really good at getting people to do what he wants. Women … he could stand by the Nenana road in winter and sell ice cubes to women, especially ones who don't know him. You'd be amazed who he's had sex with."

Had sex with. Abruptly I thought of Francine, the lonely schoolteacher. Jerry had sure sold her an ice cube or two.

"These fellows did not walk all the way out here from Clear," called William from behind, yanking me back into the chilly moment. "I will wager there is another vehicle nearby—a snow machine." He was right. A few more minutes of stumbling up the drifted trail revealed an arrangement of willow poles tied between two trees, covered with a white tarp that blended seamlessly into the surrounding snowscape.

"Invisible from the air," said Andy.

"I don't get it," I said. "Who cares?"

"Ho, ho," trumpeted William, "who cares, indeed! A government radar installation, part of a chain that stretches from the Atlantic to the Bering Sea? Who cares? Well …"

"Air patrols?" said Andy.

"Yes," said William, smiling broadly.

"Is this about spies again?" I asked.

"Yes," he said, still smiling, but a bit less enthusiastically.

"Are you a spy?" I asked him. And I admit that my hand closed around the handle of the stubby .38, still warm in the wreckage of my pocket.

"Yes, I am," he said, and glancing at my gun pocket held up his hands half jokingly. "Do not shoot." Fleetingly, I weighed the possibilities and the risks of trusting him. I've seen my movies. Spies are trained to kill. Then with an inward mental sigh, I took my hand back out of my pocket and waved his hands down.

"How did you know?" he asked.

"You're a spy?" said Andy incredulously. "You work for Washington? I thought you were a janitor at the school."

"I am," said William, "but …"

"Moscow," I said. "Right, William?"

"Moscow..." said Andy. "That doesn't make any sense. That'd mean you're a Russian spy, and that ..."

"You are correct," said William. "I am a Russian spy." I had never seen Andy at such a loss.

"That means you're the enemy," he said.

"It means," said William, "that I am William, your friend. I am the janitor at the school, and with this one exception, I am everything I ever claimed to be, which I hope you can believe." William turned his gaze back to me. "How did you figure it out?"

"It just finally added up," I said. "Maybe it was all the different ways you found to arrange the four of us around the truck at the Clear dump—with all the radar construction in the background." I looked into his clear eyes. "So, are you the enemy? Do you mean us harm?"

He sort of 'humphed' a laugh. "They sent me here just after the war," he said. "I am what they call a "mole" in the espionage business."

"A mole?" said Andy. "Like a small rodent that digs?" He was now thoroughly confused.

"Some might say rodent," said William, a bit ruefully. "I would say 'an agent from another country' who digs in, right in your midst. Someone who is with you but not of you. Not unlike yourself," he said to Andy, in a kinder voice, although I didn't get his meaning.

"For nearly ten years I had nothing to report, and you may laugh, but I woke up one morning, years ago, to find I had become American, at least in my own mind, and that I rather liked the notion. All was well until someone had the bright idea of installing all this radar up here. For my purposes, I was simply hiding out here, and happy to be. But now it is all changed. There are secrets here, and back in Moscow, people insisting that it is my job to find out those secrets and ship them back to the motherland. But what I found was that someone else was seeking that same information."

"What?" said Andy. "Another Russian spy?"

"Not ours," said William.

"How can you be sure?" I asked.

He gave me a look. "Because I am a very good spy, and because my sister's brother is the head of my branch. That is how I got such a comfortable assignment in the first place. And he is very well entrenched. If there were another spy, he would know—and I would know. The fact is," he said, "I do know where these spies are coming from, I am just not sure I know why."

"Where?" I said.

"From America," he said. "American spies are stealing classified information and offering it for sale to the highest bidder. In this case, I believe the high bidder was represented by those two East German gentlemen."

"But how?" I asked. "How does it work?"

"Something to do with Frankie," said William. "But you've probably guessed that, too." I nodded.

"But why?" said Andy.

"Now that," said William, "is the question, is it not? Cash, I suppose. I am pretty sure who is taking the information, and how they are getting it off the base."

"That would be the man calling himself Masterson," I said.

"Right again," said William.

"I'm guessing he had a change of heart," I said, "and thought he could get back what he sold that ended up with Frankie."

"*That's* why he was so desperate," said Andy. "But how does Frankie figure into all this?"

"I think they were using Frankie as a pipeline," said William. "But I have been unable to determine how, exactly."

"But why Frankie?" said Andy. "He wasn't spy material. He was a dumbshit. Had been all his life."

"He was greedy," said William, "and willing to sell out anybody for the right price."

"And expendable," I added. "If something goes wrong, Frankie is easy to eliminate and everybody will just say he got what he deserved. Which may be what happened."

In the far distance, one shot fired and then another, and the sounds seemed to hang together in the brittle air for a long time. We listened, nothing moving but the vapors of our warm breath.

"That is not good," said William.

"A hunter?" said Andy.

"Hunter of what, is the problem," said William. He turned his attention to the snow machine. I had never seen anything like it. We had all seen the big arctic Sno-Cats with cabs on top to carry four or more. This was about the size of a large motorcycle—but thicker—made to carry two or possibly three in a pinch. It was sort of pumpkin colored, and blunt nosed, with a pair of skis protruding from beneath the front cowling. Scripted below the windscreen was the name 'Polaris.'

"What makes it go?" I asked.

"Here," said William, pointing to the back of the machine. "A track. Help me push this out of the shadow." We did, and it was heavier than it looked.

"I studied such machines in espionage academy," said William, dropping to one knee, squinting at the engine. "I was very good at the academy—top of my class—which is why I got this 'plum' assignment."

"Chandelar?" said Andy. We exchanged glances.

"Oh yes," said William. "Many of my classmates were sentenced to lives in New York City and Washington D.C., where secrets are actually kept—and there is a certain element of risk and danger. I asked my sister's brother to send me to some out-of-the-way place where I could blend in."

"Well," said Andy, "that's Chandelar!" He watched William poke at the engine, and dug impatiently up his sleeve to look at his wristwatch. He dropped to one knee beside William. "What are you looking for?"

"A switch," said William. "It may be hidden. I may have to hot-wire it."

"There's a key on the dash," said Andy.

"Oh," said William, rising.

Andy stood up, too. "You sure you were first in that class?" said Andy.

"Machines, not so much, but I received very high marks for invisible inks."

"So even if we can't get it started, we can tell if there are any secret messages written on it?"

"Sarcasm, this is a whole new side of you, Andy," said William.

"Sorry," said Andy. "Those shots. I think they're more trouble. If we can't get this thing running …"

William turned the key in the ignition, grasped the wooden pull-cord handle and gave it a yank. *Chuff!* went the machine. William adjusted something. "Needs a little choking," he said, and pulled again. The engine fired once, lagged, fired again, then caught and held, building to a high-pitched ragged idle, filling the immediate area with a dense cloud of gas-rich exhaust that socked in around us like a fog, refusing to either rise or dissipate.

"Did they teach you how to drive one of these in spy school," asked Andy.

"Indubitably," said William, and straddled the smoking beast, motioning for the two of us to squeeze behind.

"In-doo-buh-*what?*" said Andy, climbing on behind William, resting his rifle stock on his right thigh, and his backpack on his left. I climbed on last and looked around for something to hang on to.

"Ever ride a motorcycle, Father," asked Andy. I shook my head. "Rode a little Vespa in Italy," he said. "Vespa means 'wasp,' because of the way they sound— a lot like this thing. Go ahead, put your arms around my waist. Probably seems a little odd to you, but it beats fallin' off. I did as he suggested but rather than holding onto him, settled for grabbing fistfuls of his parka.

"It has a clutch like a motorcycle," William shouted over his shoulder and over the din of the engine. He must have found the throttle then, and backed it down to a dull roar. Grabbing one handlebar he depressed a lever, then let it out while twisting the other handle. With a jerk, the snow machine lurched forward, going from standing still to hustling along at about dogsled speed almost instantly. If I hadn't been holding on to Andy's parka, I'd still be back by the burning boat, sprawled in a snowdrift. This was better, though immediately colder.

To go north, back to town, we first had to follow the mostly snow-drifted trail west for several miles to cross a narrow channel of the Tanana and get us off the sandbar. Two snowmobiles in and only one out ahead of us, was all the traffic this trail had seen lately. As a result, drifts slanted in from one side or the other, and we tilted and sloughed, climbed, fell and shook our way along. Climbing a slight rise through a willow thicket, we flushed a pair of fully white winter ptarmigans, and spotted the channel cut of the Tanana just ahead.

"Hold on," shouted William. We could see the bank was steep here, with perhaps a thirty-foot slant to river ice. I hadn't thought about the machine having a brake. So far, we hadn't needed one, but as we topped the riverbank shoulder and started down, I was conscious of William kicking the brake while working the handlebar controls. Down we went, and I remember thinking it was much faster than we should be going.

A rope, stretched tight between willow trees on either side of the trail, cleared the cowling, catching William hard across the chest, plowing him backwards into the two of us, pitching us all off the snowmobile and into the snow. A short length of willow log, well planted midtrail, caught the front of the speeding snowmobile, flipping it twice before it hit below on a section of glare river ice and bent nearly in two, the engine chuffing a final time or two upside-down in a drift where it had come to rest.

Silence rushed back, welcome, but for the sound of William moaning. "My ribs," he gasped."

CHAPTER 29

"This is Jerry's work," said Andy, "which means he didn't head home on the river trail. He left us to die, then hustled his butt across this island to set a trap. But why? Far as he knew, we were hunks of crisp meat back at the barbecue." He aimed a well-gloved thumb at the column of black smoke still visible against the perfect blue bowl of uninterrupted sky. Then he gave me a meaningful look. "I get it. The ambush was for them, his partners! He had no way of knowing it would be us coming this way. This must be how good ol' Jerry ties up loose ends."

He knelt to gently press William's shoulders back flat on the snow. "Stay put old spy," he said, soothingly. "We're only in a little bit of trouble right now, but if you put one of your ribs through a lung, things get worse fast." Fishing for his belt under his parka he came up with a long hunting knife, flipping it neatly, catching the tip, he presented me the handle. "Start cutting long willow poles, Father," he said, "so we can drag his Roosky ass back to Chandelar and call the cavalry."

"You can't," muttered William. "Too dangerous and too slow."

"You're in better shape than me," I said, "so I could head for town and you could start dragging William." Andy nodded a time or two, considering.

188

"No," he said. "Still too dangerous. Jerry sets another trap and you're more likely to walk right into it. I think I've got to go." He took his knife back. "You stay here. Don't even bother dragging him. I'll get back to town, and get somebody with a sled back here in a couple of hours. You're both dressed for it. And even if Jerry came back this way, he wouldn't be able to make much of a play against this old guy and his spy rifle."

"Old?" muttered William, half rising. "Maybe you two boys should just hunker down here and I will crawl back to town, put a bullet in Jerry's ear, and send help."

"Easy," said Andy, gently pushing him flat again. "I'm just kidding around here. Don't get yourself all excited and puncture something."

"You both go," said William from the ground. "I am good here. If trouble comes, I can take care of myself. I am not too damaged to aim and shoot. I was trained for this, you know. About time I put it to some good use. You go on."

"He's right," said Andy.

"But …" I said.

"And the longer we stand around jawin' about it, the farther ahead Jerry gets."

"Okay," I said, and took off my pack. "Sweater in here, army blanket, some of those pilot breads with peanut butter, and extra gloves."

William hesitated. "You should not travel without your pack," he said.

"Two hours, I'm home."

"Okay," he said. "But take the food, you will need it. I will be glad for extra warmth, though."

A couple more minutes spent getting William wrapped in the blanket, concealed a bit, and made as comfortable as possible, and we were on our way down the steep bank to river ice. We had agreed that Andy would walk ahead several hundred yards and I would pay attention to just two hand signals. It was important to keep it simple, Andy said. One hand held up meant stop. One hand motioning down meant take cover. Andy was signaling now, but it wasn't either of the ones we rehearsed. This one was more like a c'mere motion, so I did. He had stopped, as though examining something, and as I drew closer I could see what— bodies of two men sprawled in the snow, their packs ransacked and nothing left of their Sno-Cat but tread tracks heading off across the ice toward Chandelar.

"I don't get it," I said. "These two took off well before us. They're the ones we heard take off before the shotgun booby trap, before the boat on fire, before Jerry whacked you and started walking for town. They would have been way ahead of him."

"Unless they stopped here and waited for him," said Andy. "Look." He rolled one of the bodies aside to reveal a collection of cigarette butts and candy wrappers in the snow. They were here awhile. Waiting for him, waiting to die and they didn't even know it, but I guess not very many of us do. They saw him coming, probably even stood up to wave at him, and he drilled them. See, nailed this one in the front and this one had started to run. He got it in the back. You think you know a guy," he said.

I felt an icy fist of fear surround my heart and begin to squeeze, making it hard to speak or even breathe.

"We've got to get back," I said. "I think this has something to do with Evie, and I think Jerry will go after her next. I think she's one of those loose ends Jerry is supposed to be taking care of. Am I wrong?"

"You're not wrong," said Andy. "That's what I think."

"She'll be alone," I said. "Unarmed."

Andy shook himself from his thoughts and began a quick, ground-covering stumble along the rough trail across the snow-drifted river ice. "Maybe alone," he called back, "but probably not unarmed. I might have mentioned to her that something like this could happen."

Suddenly I was jogging to catch up. "Breathe through your nose," Andy called back, and through your muffler. This isn't the time to frost your lungs."

Closer, I said, "You told Evie that something like this could happen? How did you know?"

"Didn't," he said. "Just like to be on the safe side if I can."

"So you didn't bring Jerry along for backup. You brought him along to keep him in sight."

"Something like that," said Andy, his warm breath carrying his words back over his shoulder in the bright, brittle air. "Of course I didn't know we were walking right into the ambush he'd arranged. Ever since that trick with the light switch and the gas can, which I remembered telling Jerry when I got back from the war. 'Course I told others too, so I couldn't be sure it was him. But things were startin' to add up. Can't say you looked very surprised about it, either."

That's when I told him about my visit with Francine. "Naked?" he said, and he whistled. "Wow. That would be something. And she has a thing going with Jerry, who's paying for her little love nest? I didn't know people really did things like that." He paused.

"And I didn't know Jerry had that kind of money to throw around. That place probably cost him thirty or forty dollars a month!" He shook his head in disbelief.

"Is Jerry coming into any kind of big money that you know about?"

"Huh?" said Andy, the question surprising him so much that he stopped in his tracks and turned. "You know the answer to that. Jerry Charlie is a Mission kid, dressed out of the mission barrel, fed at a long, trough-like table with all the rest of us Injuns. Jerry doesn't have a pot to piss in, and won't." He hesitated. "Sorry, Father," we said in unison.

"Francine thinks he's about to collect," I said. In fact, she thinks the money is overdue. Thinks its worrying poor, hard-working, earnest Jerry." And I told Andy what Francine had said about the two of them moving to Sausalito, buying a little business they could work together, having a yard, a flower garden and a picket fence.

"Oooooh," said Andy, "a picket fence. That's definitely Jerry. I'm not sure he even knows what a picket fence is. And I'm not sure he really knows where Sausalito is, or even California." We started walking again. "He's always had a way with women," said Andy, "but this time he's the *champeen.*"

After having walked most of the rest of the way lost in our own thoughts, we were climbing up from the river ice, crossing the railroad tracks, and leaving the dog-sled trail for the hard-packed, ice-glazed streets of Chandelar. A few minutes more of hard walking brought us to Frankie's cabin and past it, the short trail through a silent, snow-drifted willow woods to Evie's cabin. Although I had known where her cabin was, I had resisted, for whatever reason, going to find it, or see it, or visit her there. Now I found myself wishing I had, and wondering if it was too late.

"Got your snub-nose?" whispered Andy.

"Yes."

"Take it out of your pocket this time," he said. He swung the sniper rifle off its shoulder strap and bolted a fresh shell into the chamber. "Look wide," he whispered. "Could be a trap."

After the bright sunlight, diffused light and shadows made it hard to see in the thicket and we stopped a minute to let our eyes adjust. I was suddenly aware of silence, deep and hard-shelled, holding out dog barks and busted-muffler trucks and the sounds of distant generators. Ahead, the trail curved around a large, bluish spruce tree and I couldn't see the cabin yet, though I knew it had to be very close, situated as it was on an otherwise undeveloped city block.

A frozen tree cracked, just at my side, and I spun with my handgun up, trigger already starting to squeeze. "No!" whispered Andy. It seemed like a shout and my heart thudded up into my throat. I managed to not fire but it was close. We went a few more steps then Andy dropped to a crouch waving, first for me to get down and then to approach. Running low, I managed to get to where he was without blasting any trees.

"Blood," he said. "There on the trail."

Over his shoulder I could see a small log cabin with a dark green painted door. A covered porch, roomy for Chandelar, was stacked nearly to the roof with firewood and an axe leaned against the doorframe. Blood, a fair puddle, stained the packed snow directly in front of the door, and then dribbled around the corner on a smaller path headed toward town. There were bullet holes in the door, two in and one out by the look of the splintered wood.

"Evie," I said, and started up from my crouch, headed at a trot for the door. "No," shouted Andy, and managed to tackle me before I got there. I tried to get free of him, to get in the door and find whatever it was I had to find, though I feared I knew. I'd certainly seen enough of Jerry's other handiwork today.

It seemed we struggled for a long time, though it was seconds, and when the door creaked and began to open, we realized at the same instant how vulnerable we were, and froze. But it was Evie who stepped out the door and saw us on the ground at her feet. She smiled and exhaled audibly. "Thank God," she said. She was wearing a chenille housecoat with longies and mukluks showing under, her hair was up in big curlers tied in a bandana, and she had a Winchester, lever action carbine in both hands, by the look of it, cocked and ready to fire. "Thought that was you," she said, weakly. "Hoped it was." We managed to climb out of our dog pile and she put down her carbine and gathered us both into her arms, kissing our cheeks and holding us for long moments, as we held her. Finally, reluctantly for my part, we stepped away.

Her attempt at a smile told the story, along with a tear that overflowed one eye and tracked down her cheek. Worried, fearful—now relieved. "Come in," she said, shivered, and turned to go back through the cabin door. Over her shoulder she said, "I hope that wasn't your idea of sneaking up. I've heard less noise from stampeding caribou. I was going to shoot you, but I already shot one guy today. I try to limit myself to one a day."

194

CHAPTER 30

"Sit," she said. "A few more minutes aren't going to make a difference to William and you two need to warm up and fuel up."

"We've got to stop Jerry," said Andy.

"Jerry's long gone, maybe an hour ago. I heard some kind of engine start up back there and drive off toward the river. Things didn't go well for him here so I'm sure he's on the run."

She swirled coffee from possibly the shiniest percolator I'd ever seen, into a bright yellow ceramic mug with two finger holes in the handle. "He knocked on the door," said Evie, "a bit after noon. I'd shuttered the windows and barred the door, so no way to ambush me. Only one door, so he had to come at me that way. I wasn't about to let him in."

"So he knocked," prompted Andy.

"Yeah, he knocked. I was ready." She nodded toward the carbine. "Shell in the chamber," she said. "Not much room on either side of the door, so I just skinnied over and pressed my back against the wall under the coat rack. He knocked again. 'Who's there?' I said. He didn't answer, just pumped the two shots though the door. You saw the holes. No way to survive that. If I'd had time to think about it, I might have just climbed under the bed and hid. But something happened to me—the noise, bullets flying around my house—a water glass there by the sink shattered. I been picking up glass all afternoon."

"So …" said Andy, patiently.

"I jumped out and fired the one shot straight through the door. He made a nasty sound, a kind of 'ohhhhhh', and a cough, and I heard a thump like he fell against the door. 'Bitch,' he said, like he was gritting his teeth, and then I heard him start away around the house, dragging something."

"I saw that," said Andy. "Looks like he was dragging his rifle stock. Maybe holding the barrel like a walking stick. You winged him for sure. Upper chest or shoulder, most likely. Quite a puddle of blood out there." A few minutes more and Andy was back on his feet, pulling his mukluks back on, checking his rifle.

"I'm coming," I said, pushing back my chair.

"No, you're gonna stay here," ordered Andy. "The two of you together, and you're gonna keep staying here together until I get back with William." He looked at us both, eyes moving from one face to the other. "If you have a problem with staying here at the cabin, then I'll walk you to the Coffee Cup and you can sit there for three or four hours until I get back."

"No," said Evie. "Rosie would have a field day, the two of us sitting there that long. We'll be fine here." She threw a look at me, maybe a bit worried. "Won't we?"

"We'll be good here," I said.

"Nice choice of words," said Andy. I admit I blushed, and they both laughed at me. "See that you are!" said Andy.

Andy bummed a waffled, long-sleeved undershirt from Evie, pulling his suspenders aside and stripping to his nearly identical shirt, then pulling

196

everything back on, buttoning and zipping himself back into his trail clothes. "William is going to be a chilly pepper by the time I get back there. Couple hours lying in the snow, not quite out of the wind, cold gets right inside you." He accepted a bundle of sandwiches from Evie, tucking one in a pocket and the rest in his sled pack.

"I made extra for William," Evie said. He nodded.

"Keep that snub-nose handy," he said to me. "I don't think you'll need it. I imagine Jerry has gone off somewhere to hide and bleed." He chanced a direct look at Evie. "Maybe to die."

She met his gaze, evenly. "He shot at me, two shots. He came to my cabin and tried to kill me. I shot back. It's the way the dice flips and I won't feel bad about it. The way I see it, if he dies, it's like he pulled the trigger on himself. I sure wouldn't have shot him if he hadn't tried to shoot me."

"Okay," said Andy. "I agree."

"Me, too," I said, though no one had asked. I retrieved my pistol out of the pocket of my parka, where I'd thrown it on the couch. I held it up for Andy to see, and he nodded.

"Keep it close," he said again. Flipping his hood up, he patted me on the shoulder, a bit awkwardly, hugged his cousin and kissed her cheek. "Stay inside," he said. "Don't take chances." They froze like that for an instant, at arms length, just looking at each other.

"You neither," said Evie. "Keep your head down."

"God speed." I said. Evie raised the bar on the door and eased the door slowly in until Andy could get a look outside. Then she opened it wide enough to slip through, and he was gone.

"Two o'clock," said Evie, checking her watch. "Maybe a half hour to harness up. If he's not back here by five, we're going after him."

I opened my mouth to say something. "Don't say it," she said, and I didn't.

We drank coffee, ate a little, oddly quiet and a little awkward as we moved in unique and uncertain orbits about the small cabin. It was the tidiest place I'd ever been. And for its size, I'd never seen a home with more books. The walls were virtually lined with volumes of all descriptions, carefully alphabetized, arranged and dusted. I remembered her first visit to my office, the first time I'd seen her, how she studied the shelves. Now I knew why.

"Read all these?" I asked.

"Yeah, every one. Some twice."

"You don't seem like the book type." She raised her eyebrows. She was sitting across the room, her kitchen table between us, watching me circle. "What type do I seem?" she asked.

"I don't know," I said, honestly at a loss. The only type I could think of, that I really didn't have the courage to tell her, was that she seemed like the 'very dear' type, at least to me.

I found myself wondering, how people who care about each other manage to dare to close the distance between them. Was it easier when I was young, or was it Mary who did the distance closing, the heavy lifting in love while I was oblivious?

One hour turned into two as we circled, sitting, rising, thumbing pages of books or magazines, talking or not talking about nothing much, with what seemed like so much left to say. Until at last, without meaning to, I pulled back a chair on my side of her kitchen table, just as she pulled back the opposite chair and we both committed ourselves to sitting, in a way that made it awkward to suddenly stand back up and move away. I looked at the sugar bowl and she seemed to be looking at a book on the shelf behind me. I looked at my coffee cup, the one I was holding in both my hands, and she turned her head to look at the kitchen sink. I looked down at the wedding ring I was still wearing, and then I looked up into her warm, coffee-brown eyes, and couldn't look away again. And didn't want to. And she began to speak.

"Something's changed in my life," Evie said, "and I didn't realize it until this morning when I thought I was about to die, when I heard Jerry's footsteps and knew he was coming to kill me. For months I've been planning and expecting my death, and making orderly arrangements to leave this life, and it all seemed," she hesitated, "somehow okay." She stretched her arms across the checked tablecloth, both of her hands reaching for both of mine. Like a spectator I watched my hands push my coffee cup aside and reach for hers, her browner, more angular wrists extending from white sleeve cuffs and our fingers entwined.

"When he got back here before you and Andy, it seemed likely—in fact it seemed nearly a sure thing—that he killed you both. And the only thing I could think of," she said, "as I was cocking the rifle, as I was pressing my back against the wall there by the door, with the coats around me, my only sorrow, that I wouldn't be seeing you again. And that part of it seemed nearly unbearable. Have you ever felt that way?" she asked me, and I hesitated.

Was this a time to be honest? About feelings? Had I never been honest about feelings before? I thought I had. Was I a priest now, or a man? Or was there a difference?

Tell her, whispered a voice, somehow Mary's voice, very gently from the far corner of a closed room in my heart. *Tell her!*

"No," I said to Evie, and I saw something in her pull back, a hopefulness recede. But then I said, "not until this morning, with the boat on fire, when a man I'd never met—certainly never wronged—pointed a gun at us and told us he was willing to burn us to death to find out what he wanted to know. And all I could think about," I said, and I saw her take a breath, and I saw the hope in her eyes, "all I could think about was the great, nearly unbearable sorrow of not seeing you again. As though I had a message for you, but I don't know what it is. As though I had a gift, but I don't know what that is, either." But then I did know, and I stood up as she stood, and stretched across the table.

Kiss her, said the voice. But I no longer needed the encouragement. I was kissing her.

CHAPTER 31

It was five seventeen by the wind-up Westclox on the sill of Evie's shuttered kitchen window when we heard Andy rapping a pre-arranged shave-and-a-haircut-plus three knocks on the door.

"About darn time," breathed Evie, disentangling herself from the warm bundle that had been us, sitting close through an afternoon that, while pleasant, at times seemed everlasting as we waited for Andy's return.

A roil of heavy, arctic air swirled at knee height nearly the length of the cabin as Andy squeezed himself quickly in, pushing the door tight behind him.

"Where's William?" Evie fluttered, waiting for him to peel himself out of his trail clothes so she could fling her arms around him.

"Delivered straight to the nurse," said Andy, unwrapping a muffler from around his neck and stooping to untie his tall mukluks. "Left her to tape up those ribs. Thought I'd better get over here and let you two know we made it back safe before you got the notion to head out on the rescue trail yourselves." He looked at me closely, then Evie, then around the room. But it doesn't look like you're standin' at the door with your parkas on."

"We were just about to," I said. "Ready for hot coffee?"

"Hours ago," he said.

With cold fingers laced around a hot mug, Andy told of the trip out. "Following Jerry's crawler tracks out of town was easy. No way to hide a set of those," he said. He followed them until they intersected the trail that led back to William. Sure enough, Andy found him in good shape, bundled down in a snowdrift out of the wind, drifting snow all but covering the extra blanket he'd tented over himself. "No worse for wear," said Andy. "That old spy wasn't even chilly."

"Spy?" said Evie, which set us off on the revelations of our morning trip.

"You didn't tell her any of this stuff?" said Andy. "You didn't tell her about that Hoot Gibson thing you done with the snub-nose? Shoulda heard him. 'I suppose there's no way of talking you out of killing us?' he says. Then bang, bang, bang! What'd you two talk about all afternoon anyway," he asked. Then he did his back and forth look again. "Never mind," he said. "Don't think I want to know."

"You shot a man?" said Evie, hand over mouth. "It must have been terrible."

"We were dead men," said Andy. "The alternative would've been really bad news. It was them or us."

I nodded. I was happy to not think about the shooting, though I suspected I couldn't hold it off forever. There hadn't been any self-defense pistol classes at seminary, either. The distance I had come from the person I thought I was and the life I thought I would be leading, was forming as a dull ache in my chest somewhere behind my heart, and I believed there would be a reckoning one day soon.

"A spy," breathed Evie again, when we'd finished the tale. And Jerry selling government secrets, I ..." she broke off, momentarily at a loss.

"This all has to do with Frankie," I said. "Maybe why he was killed, and maybe how he got somehow connected to the spy business and ..." I hesitated. "Which means that some of this must also have something to do with you."

She nodded, smiled a small, grim smile and dropped her eyes.

I admit I felt bad, even duplicitous. After kissing her and sitting closely with her these past few hours, then asking hard questions seemed especially awkward and cold-hearted.

"I'm sorry," I said. "I ..."

"No, you're right. Frankie has been killed. These other men have been killed. You and Andy were nearly ..." She squeezed her eyes tight and a tear rolled down each cheek. She blinked her eyes open and looked at each of us. "Ask me what you need to," she said.

She didn't know who killed Frankie. Like the rest of the town, she could have made a list of people who said they'd like to. She had worked for him since the day he plucked her out of the mission school. "He was actually pretty good to me," she said.

"Good to you!" exclaimed Andy. "You've got to be kidding. He used you."

"The truth is," she said, "if anybody got used, it probably wasn't me."

"He made you into a ... a ... prostitute!"

Evie looked down at her hands, now folded in her lap. "Actually," she said, "he made me into a bookkeeper, his an accountant. He made me a partner, sent me to New York to school, listened to my ideas. I was never a prostitute. In fact I'm nearly a virgin at thirty-two." Andy and I exchanged glances as her cheeks reddened.

"He was illiterate. Couldn't read, couldn't write."

"Wait a minute," said Andy. "His place is full of expensive-looking books. What were those for? Who read them?"

Evie smiled ruefully. "He had me order them, all expensive editions, so he'd look like somebody who could read. I read some of them, the ones I didn't already own. They were just for show. It was all just for show. He used to make up stories about himself, to spread around, about how smart he was or how tough, but most of it wasn't true."

"We found a contract, to murder someone. That seemed pretty real."

"Yeah, it was," she said. "He was careful to keep that from me, though I did all the filing, so was bound to see it and know about it. I didn't write that!" she said, her eyes flicking from Andy's to mine.

"So who did the shooting?" asked Andy.

"I didn't know at the time, but after all this, I'm pretty sure it was Jerry."

"That's what I think," said Andy. "That explains the extra cash Jerry had to throw around."

"What I don't understand," I said, "is what Frankie actually did to earn a living."

"It changed over time," she said. "Mostly lending money at really terrible rates. He started out plundering the local people and over time I got him to plunder people from out of town, which was more

204

profitable and less likely to have somebody from right here shoot him."

"So Frankie's will, the inheritance to the church—to me—that was all you?"

"Yes," she said evenly.

"And the handwriting in the will," I said, "was a perfect match with the ledgers because it was you who wrote everything." She nodded. "So none of that is legal," I said.

"Actually, it is," she said. "Well, mostly. Frankie and I were legally partners with rights of survivorship. It seemed easier and cleaner to just sign it all over to you, knowing that you would find ways to help people here and get the money back to folks who really needed it."

"His business partner," said Andy, with a pained expression. "So you had something to do with getting him hooked up with these spies?"

She shook her head. "I don't know what that's about, or where it came from. He kept it from me, maybe to protect me or maybe to just have an idea that was solely his. After a while, he got pretty resentful about me being 'the boss.' One thing I can tell you. He collected two piles of cash that I saw and later counted, that added up to one hundred and twenty thousand dollars."

Andy gasped. "One hundred and twenty thousand dollars? That's more money than President Eisenhower makes in a year!"

I thought of my own salary, just under two thousand dollars a year. "No wonder they were willing to kill us to find out whatever it was they needed to find out. It was a fortune."

"Frankie was in way over his head," said Andy. He looked at Evie, maybe a bit sharply.

"I never knew," she insisted. "I never saw this coming. All of a sudden he's having secret meetings, brings home this pile of cash, and gets unbelievably cheerful. Oh and, you know what else?"

"What?" said Andy and I, nearly as one.

"That's when he had me order a camera and lights, and all that darkroom stuff. Next thing I knew, he was taking photographs of anybody he could get naked in there. It was," she hesitated and shuddered, "horrible. And I refuse to believe anybody would give him a hundred grand for any of the pictures I saw."

"So he was never interested in photography before that?" I asked.

"Never."

"Maybe he just never had the money before," ventured Andy.

She shook her head. "Frankie was never interested in anything but making money and making himself look like a big guy. No hobbies, no vices—he never smoked or chewed—just whatever he had to do to make a legend of himself. So he was certainly never interested in taking pictures. And I had to read the manual to him so he could learn to work in the darkroom. At first I thought the darkroom would be something else that I would end up doing for him. Ugh. All those poor, wretched, naked women. But no, he didn't even want me around, once he had the hang of it. I even thought it might be some kind of sex thing, but never saw him interested in that, either. Well, until he started taking pictures of Roberta. That was interesting. It was like he was in eighth grade again. I started to feel like his mom."

"Jerry was sure interested in those photographs," said Andy. We sat quiet for a few moments. I didn't know what the others were thinking, but I was thinking about Jerry. How he started out as a mission kid, and now possibly ended up dying alone in the cold, a murderer, with a bullet in him.

"I wonder if Jerry's dead?" said Andy.

"I hope so," said Evie. "I want this all to be over."

I didn't say anything, but didn't—for a moment—think it was all over.

CHAPTER 32

From Fairbanks, the Bishop's secretary called me early the next morning. The Bishop would be visiting on Sunday, in four days time, she had said. The fact that the Bishop didn't call me himself, as he had on several previous occasions, only served to support my sense that all was not right with the world.

The secretary, Rosemary, cool and efficient, often with lips pressed together, closed our conversation by saying, "I hope you'll have a good turnout."

Normally, the Bishop's visitation would assure a good turnout, if there were time to let people know he would be coming. Church attendance had been neither better nor worse lately, but I was left with the vague sense of not exactly doing my job, which was never that well defined anyway.

When I told Andy about the visit, he only raised his eyebrows. "Good timing," he said.

"I like the Bishop," was what Evie said. "I'll be there."

I was sleepless during much of that night, and found myself going over 'things done and things left undone' as the Prayer Book says. It seemed that most of what I'd been doing lately was breaking and entering, concealing evidence of crimes—including murder— plus I'd been barroom brawling, and shooting people.

None of those things were normally found in the job description of young mission priests.

What I had also been doing: finding and absolving Frankie's many victims, enlisting them where possible as part of my 'prayer brigade' for Evie, visiting with Mr. and Mrs. Big Scotty Neilson—and scaring him off his deathbed—in addition to consorting with a really decent woman who was known locally as a prostitute, and a really naked woman, known locally as a school teacher—who wanted to 'heal' me with sex—seemed to have occupied the bulk of my working hours. It all left me feeling somehow unworthy and like my unworthiness would be clearly apparent to a visiting bishop, my boss.

As to Jerry, he disappeared. It was as though he suddenly turned to light, dry snowflakes and blew away. Following the tread trail of the Sno-Cat, even after a light snowfall and some drifting, was easy for Andy. They found it abandoned, tank empty, about twenty miles away. Dog-sledding a tank of diesel out from town, and building a small fire under the engine block, soon had it started and driven back to Chandelar. Parked on the main street, it was claimed by security staff from Clear within several days. "These guys get liquored up and 'borrow' them," was the explanation.

"Found it out on the river," reported Andy. "A big slick of glare ice, blown clear of snow for miles. He could walk or crawl away in any direction and leave no trail. And this is something Jerry is really good at. I'm good, but I'm not sure I could find him. Or if I did find him, not sure he wouldn't put a bullet in me before I could enjoy my success. With any luck, he's bled out or froze solid by now." Andy hesitated. "But I wouldn't count on it."

I admit that midwinter days in Chandelar were hard for me, anyway. With the river frozen solid, temperatures in the mid-minus thirties, and only about four hours of full daylight, I felt as low and slow as songbirds I would occasionally find, clinging to frozen branches. With their feathers puffed out for warmth, their heart rates slowed nearly to stopping, they couldn't run, couldn't hide, didn't care if I walked up and touched them. And now, especially in anticipation of the Bishop's visit, I felt pretty much that way myself.

I also found myself feeling resentful and probably a little sorry for myself. *I've put myself way out on a cold limb for these people,* I found myself thinking—staying with my cold bird metaphor—*and now this.* I began to imagine the two of us, the Bishop and me, come this Sunday, waiting in the church vestibule to greet the flock, only to find no flock. The more I pictured it, the worse it all became, and I began to think of starting to pack.

"You okay?" asked Andy, Friday morning over coffee.

"No," I said.

He straightened in his chair, gripping his coffee mug more firmly. "Wanna talk about it?" he asked.

I didn't. I shook my head. There was nothing I could say to him at this point that wouldn't sound like whining. "Bishop stuff," I said. It was all I could say.

He nodded as if that made sense. "Ahhh," he said.

While I wasn't paying attention, November had given way to December. The previous Wednesday had been the anniversary of the surprise attack on Pearl Harbor. In 1941, I was still living at home in Kentucky, and had been cleaning up the basement as directed by my father. The oil furnace kept it warm down there, and I'd spent a mindless hour rearranging preserved fruit on fruitroom shelves and boxing up garden potatoes, heaped on the concrete floor after a late September harvest. President Roosevelt was speaking as I came up the stairs, and my parents were mesmerized in front of the Philco. I might have thought the President had died, except that I was hearing his voice. I'd never heard of Pearl Harbor. Most people hadn't. We sure knew where it was after that.

A surprise attack. That's what this thing with Jerry was. And the more I thought about it, the more the Bishop's visit began to feel the same way.

Saturday night I went to bed early and couldn't sleep. Just after one o'clock, Mary came gliding into my room. *Buck up,* she said.

"I'm bucked!" was all I could say in my defense.

Funny, she said. She was still wearing the sheer nightie, but I was almost too distracted to leer. *This isn't your biggest problem. In fact, if you weren't so busy feeling sorry for yourself, it wouldn't be a problem at all.*

I sat up. "More trouble coming?" I said, but the bluish light had gone out and the room was empty. I heard her answer but it came from my lips. "You know there is."

I was waiting on the riverbank at sunrise, about ten thirty, when the Bishop's Cessna did a smooth river landing and taxied on skis to where I sat in the Frankie memorial truck with the heater on.

We shook hands and he smiled a little, which helped. I took a line and tied one wing to a concrete-filled oil barrel while he did the same on the other end, and we drove in relative silence the five minutes across the tracks and down the street to the church.

"Nice truck," said the Bishop. "You must have really made an impression on Frankie."

"Never met him," I said.

The Bishop leaned back to look at me, kind of angling his head. His eyes, reflecting the incredible bowl of absolutely cloudless sky, were pure bright blue. "Sometimes, it gets down to the end and people just have a change of heart," he said.

"Frankie?"

He considered for a moment. "Nah."

In our vestments, we waited together in the vestibule as the minutes ticked slowly up to eleven o'clock. A couple of people trickled in. First came the organist and the acolyte, and then the public health nurse and her husband.

"How is William?" I asked.

"Cranky," she replied, "but he'll knit."

The Bishop raised his eyebrows, inviting details. "William Stolz," I said.

"Janitor at the school," said the Bishop, nodding.

"Broke some ribs in a snowmobile accident," I said.

"Ahhh," said the Bishop.

At eleven straight up, I rang the bell, pulling the rope slowly and deliberately to give people a last-minute opportunity to show up and not be late. The bell rings in sets of two for regular service, with single rings saved for funerals. It didn't seem to matter how slowly I rang. The door didn't open and people didn't come in. It was my dream all over again, only now I had no

Mary to show up and advise me, and no covers to put my head under.

"Better get started," said the Bishop.

The first organ notes sounded as we came through the doors, and the first lines of the hymn were just the five or six voices against the relative thunder of the elderly pump organ. Facing the altar, I didn't see them begin to arrive, but I heard the other voices, and through subsequent verses and refrains, I heard—and felt—the swell of men and women, and even children as their voices took up the words and the ancient melody of Advent, until on the final 'amen' when I turned to face the congregation, we had become a mighty voice.

I was stunned. Every pew was filled. Folding chairs had been opened in the back and all were occupied. Everyone was there: Andy, Evie, Mr. and Mrs. Big Scotty, Molly with her new baby, Rosie Jimmy from the Coffee Cup, William—and nearly everybody I'd called on Frankie's list. I couldn't help but smile and when I looked at the Bishop. He was smiling, too.

"Let us give thanks," I began, from my heart.

CHAPTER 33

"I really think he's dead," said Evie, sipping her coffee and warming her hands on her blue mug.

Weeks had passed with neither sight nor word of Jerry. For all of Alaska's size, it was still close-knit, with trappers, dogsledders, the military, and the Territorial police, crisscrossing the wild valleys. And with more bush pilots per capita than nearly any place in the world, there were plenty of eyes in the sky. It also helped that we were all always nearly ravenous for news. It was not considered strange at all to slide into a chair at the Coffee Cup and hear somebody say they heard that somebody had seen somebody over near the Twenty-mile Trail. But so far, none of those 'somebodies' was Jerry.

"But you're still locking your door," said Andy.

"Yeah."

"Good girl," he said. "Smart."

"But I resent having to lock my door," said Evie. "First time in my whole life, except when I lived in New York. Then I locked all my locks. My apartment door had five different locks on it!"

"Why live in a place like that?" said Andy.

"If I have to lock my door here," she said, "what's the difference?"

Christmas, with all its celebration, services, and responsibilities had come and gone. Advent purple had given way to crimson and I resented having to lock my doors, too. In retrospect, one of the reasons I came here probably had to do with not needing to lock my doors.

Today, Saturday, was New Year's Eve. The day dawned reluctantly, resentfully, with gusting winds, blowing snow and temperatures near forty below. Early coffee was less early than usual, with Andy straggling in at about nine and Evie shortly thereafter.

"Overslept," he grinned as he struggled out of his gear. "Stayed up late reading a picture book from the library. *Life On the Mediterranean*, it's called, twenty-two pages of color photos. I'm so primed to go, I spent nearly an hour building a new budget and figuring my savings."

"So when are you going?" I asked him.

"Let's see. This is almost 1956," he said, fiddling with his fingers as though counting. "I should get there about the turn of the next century!" He laughed. "Think there'll still be a world in the year 2000? Probably all blown to hell with an A-bomb, and me still tryin' to get back to Italy." It was a good day to not have to be out, and we three sat around the table, comfortable, sipping and talking while looking out the window at blowing snow.

It was our usual wide-ranging conversation. Politics, religion, science and sports, not necessarily in that order. Somehow we got back on the topic of life in the mission school.

"One time," said Andy, "Frankie, Jerry and me got out with the twenty-two rifle. We were supposed to be bringin' back grouse for the kitchen."

"Supposed to?" said Evie. "That doesn't sound good. What were you doing?"

"We were out by the railroad, and there was a sign there about something. I don't even remember

215

what. It was a pretty long message, maybe four or five sentences with periods and commas and stuff, and I think it was Frankie, got the big idea of replacing all the punctuation with bullet holes. But it had to be neat! Frankie was a lousy shot, so Jerry and I took turns shooting them out. One that missed owed the other a quarter."

"So who won?" I asked.

He gave me a mock scathing look. "Let's just say that I was able to buy candy bars for all three of us at the store, and have nickels left over to clink in my pocket."

"So who did win?" asked Evie, provoking him. And it was while they were bantering back and forth, that I began to imagine the sign with the periods shot out, and was pretty sure I figured out what Jerry and the others had been willing to kill for.

~

There's always a New Year's Eve dance in Chandelar, and just about everybody who can walk turns out for it. There are the old people, tribal elders among them, adults and children, and everybody has a good time.

In the gymnasium-sized Civic Center they had rigged a fat-spindled 45-rpm phonograph with a PA microphone for extra volume in front of the speaker. Everybody danced. I'm not a natural dancer, but I danced with children—some standing on my feet—with teens and with adults. Then, with midnight upon us, Patti Page was launched, singing "Tennessee Waltz" and the countdown began: ten, nine, eight …

At precisely midnight, a tremendous cheer momentarily drowned out the music and people began kissing each other. I'd never seen anything quite like it.

Rosie Jimmy, who I had suspected of being sweet on me, kissed me. I felt a tug on my sleeve and turned to find Rosie's grandmother, Violet Jimmy, who had made casseroles to keep me from starving those first few months. She wore a flowered scarf tied tightly around her head, and her wrinkled face was set in a loving smile.

"You're here for a kiss, too?" I said to her. *Like grandmother like granddaughter*, I thought, but I was mistaken. She shook her head emphatically.

"Not me," she said. "This one!" And she pulled on a sleeve she held tightly, dragging the victim into view. It was Evie, laughing, blushing—probably wishing she could make herself disappear.

"Should we?" I asked her. "The whole town is here."

She looked around at the crowd. "You still think we're much of a secret?"

"Maybe not," I admitted, and put my arms around her, and we kissed, and we danced to "Tennessee Waltz" in each other's arms. Outside, the new year blew in as a blizzard out of Siberia, snow pelting sideways and drifts already obliterating roads and trails, with sled dogs curled up and hunkered down, cozy, completely buried in the snow.

All the while we were warm and dry and happy, and danced as though we hadn't a care—or an enemy— in the whole wide world.

CHAPTER 34

The icy tip of the gun barrel woke me. It was pressed against the side of my head. I hadn't heard the window glass break in my back door, nor the latch rattle. In the bluish, moonlit room I had no trouble recognizing Jerry and behind him, hands bound in front of her, Evie.

"Up," said Jerry, making a similar up movement with the gun barrel. I began to think of things I might do to turn the tables. I knew he'd been recently wounded, was probably not fully recovered. So many plans converged in my lately sleeping brain that I did nothing. "Don't," said Jerry, as if sensing my thoughts, and he backed out of immediate range.

I got up as directed and turned on no lights, also as directed. With the two standing, watching me, I got dressed. "Parka," said Jerry, "and mitts. You're gonna need to be warm for awhile." I turned to Evie and our eyes met. "None of that," said Jerry.

When I was fully dressed and ready to go, Jerry moved to stand directly in front of me and pointed his handgun, a military-type .45 automatic, directly at Evie's face. "No time to play games," he said. "I been all through this place, pretty sure you're not hiding the photos here. I'm gonna ask you once. Where are they?" He thumbed back the hammer on the .45. "Won't ask again," he said.

"Don't tell him," said Evie.

"Shut up, Eve," he said. "Father is going to tell me now, aren't you? Because if he doesn't, he knows he has to watch you die, and then still cough up the photos. Right, Father?"

I nodded. "Behind the altar."

"See how easy that was?" I could see him smile a tight smile in the semi-darkness, not the disarming, goofy Jerry grin I had grown accustomed to.

"Can I ask a question?"

"Shoot," he said, then laughed at his joke. "Like you could." Then he looked at me seriously. "What do you wanna know?" he said.

"Did you kill Frankie?" I asked.

"Me? Heck no. Frankie was my friend, sort of." He turned to Evie. "I thought you killed Frankie."

"I didn't," said Evie. "And I didn't start out thinking you did, but …"

"But now you do."

"I guess not if you say you didn't," she said.

"I do say," Jerry said, then turned to me. "Come on, let's get those photos."

"The microdots are gone," I said. "I brushed them all into the fire."

"Shit," said Jerry. "That's what it was? Microdots? That crazy Frankie! Tell me how you figured it," he said, like we were friends chatting over coffee.

"Andy told me about you two shooting out the periods on the railroad sign," I told him. I remembered reading about microdots during the last war. They used to put them onto documents in place of the periods."

"That's crazy," said Jerry. "No periods on those photos. No words."

219

"No, but the way the allies found them in the war was that they were shiny. I mean they were tiny photos of secrets. So what better thing to put them on than other photos. Especially when most of the people who look at the photos would be distracted by the naked women."

"They're all gone?"

"I did my best," I told him.

"Shit! Do you know how much money you just cost me?"

"One hundred and twenty thousand?"

That stopped him. "I was only expecting sixty thousand. Oh," he said, and turned again to Evie, "forgot you'd have a share." Now Jerry turned the pistol on me, confronting her directly. "Where will I find all this cash?" he asked her, again thumbing back the hammer for emphasis.

"Under my cabin floor," she said, "under the sink."

"One more question," I said.

"Sure, but hurry, we've got some traveling to do before daylight."

"You're going to kill us."

"Not a question," he said, "but yes. You two are dead, just still walking around."

"You're going to shoot us?"

"Heck no. I mean, not if I can help it. I mean, you bein' a priest and all, and Evie from the Mission. Nah. I don't want to shoot you, but it doesn't mean I don't want you to die. Oh," he said, "and Andy, too. You're probably already thinkin' Andy is going to rescue you. Funny thing is, that's what he'll be thinkin' too. Won't help." He rotated his body just a little, enough to show me the sniper rifle hanging from its shoulder strap. "Won't help a bit." He peered at my bedside windup clock. "Gotta get going. Guess we'll leave those photos. No good to me now."

"Oh," he said, "almost forgot." He dug in his pocket for a piece of paper and a pencil that he handed to Evie. "You're gonna leave a note for Andy, an invitation actually. No warnings, though he might figure it out anyway. Just write, Meet us on the river behind the Mission." He paused. "Write this, too: Have big news. And make sure to put—what are those things? Oh yeah, an exclamation mark." He laughed. "Been waiting to shoot him for so long."

We left the note on the kitchen table, weighted by a coffee mug. Andy would come after us, I knew that. But he would come carefully and armed, because he had been warned. He and I both knew Evie's writing and this wasn't it. Andy would be receiving this message from a dead man. It was written in Frankie's hand.

We eased out the front door, so as not to wake the sled dogs, and single file started down the snow-packed road toward the old Mission. What to do? I thought of shouting 'run' and both of us sprinting off in different directions. Jerry was good, but was he good enough to shoot both of us in motion, with a handgun? It didn't matter. He was good enough to hit one of us and I was afraid it would be Evie, which seemed too huge a risk.

Someone was walking toward us. I could just see him in the ice-foggy gloom. Jerry saw him, too. He moved closer behind me. "Say more than 'good morning' to this guy and he dies. It's on your hands. Think of it as protecting another member of your flock."

221

The space between us closed. I could recognize him, Isaac Evan, headed down to fuel up the town generator. Evie was in the lead. Would he notice her hands were bound? Would he think it strange that the Mission priest was out before dawn with these two? Would he call anyone, or tell anyone? Would he say 'Hey, what's going on here?'

He wouldn't. He didn't. He went softly by. "Good morning," he said, and we each said 'good morning' to him, and then he was falling away behind and we were walking out in a misty dawn to die.

I thought of Mary, of course. I always thought of Mary. I thought of Evie, too. Could I save her? I stopped in the road and turned to Jerry, who stopped abruptly and pointed the .45 at my face. It made me want to close my eyes or duck out of the way, as though that would help.

"Let her go," I said. "You don't need her. You've got me. She doesn't have to die."

"Touching," said Jerry. "She said all those things too. Don't really need either of you now that the microdots are gone. You were telling the truth about that, weren't you, Father?"

"Afraid so," I said.

"You woulda died anyway, so it doesn't make a lot of difference." He motioned with the gun. "Keep walking."

Lights had begun to blink on in cabins as we reached the outskirts of the village proper. Beyond there, the road paralleled the railroad tracks for about a mile, then continued straight where the tracks turned to head off north toward Nenana. Soon we were crunching up the birch lane toward the Mission, and as I caught my first glimpse of that old, haunted place, I realized the sky had already begun to lighten into another bright, perfectly clear day.

Evie swung out of line and turned. "Can I have my hands untied," she said. "No blood flow, I think they're starting to freeze."

Jerry grinned at her. "Sure," he said. "Wouldn't want Princess to freeze her little hands." He nodded at me. "Go ahead and untie her."

As we passed the Mission, I studied the darkened windows. There were stories of faces the townspeople had seen through these panes, faces of those long dead. Would I see them now? Could they help me save us? I didn't think so. But it didn't matter because I saw no faces, dead or alive. I thought of Jerry's joke, now so long ago: do we have a prayer?

Some priest, I thought, disgusted. I walked all the way out here to die and it never occurred to me to pray. I began to wonder if I'd entered the wrong profession. Maybe mission priest work wasn't what I was supposed to do. I must have slowed. From behind me Jerry said, "Not here, we're headed out on the river."

The going was rougher as the meager trail ended and we continued on through drifted snow, anywhere from ankle to thigh deep. The riverbank was high here, but Jerry knew a slant of beach that put us uneventfully to the river ice in the strengthening predawn. The Tanana was more than a half mile wide here, an expanse blown nearly clear of snow. There was nowhere to hide, nowhere to even hunker down out of the insistent, knifelike cold of a steady breeze out of the north. That's when I realized Jerry was bringing us to a place that would force Andy out into his rifle sights, from any direction. Sure enough, midriver we stopped.

I looked around the place I would die. Instinctively, I reached out to Evie and pulled her to my side. "Let her walk away," I said to Jerry.

"Shut up," he responded, then took a long slow look around, nodding his head, satisfied. "This will do," he said finally. Then he looked at us directly. "Take off your clothes."

"We'll freeze," said Evie.

"Yeah," said Jerry, and for the first time this morning, grinned his goofy Jerry grin and laughed. "You bet you will," he said. "You remember Rudy Fredrickson," he said to Evie, like they were reminiscing over a beer.

"Yeah," she said, hesitantly, "he disappeared."

Jerry laughed again. "He sure did. Frankie was with me when I staked him out here, chained him up like a husky—in his long johns—windier that day," he said. "He was down and nearly dead in about an hour. Still had a little, tiny heartbeat when I shot him." Listening to Jerry, we had stopped moving, which he suddenly realized. "Undress," he said again, "down to your longies." He switched his gaze from Evie to me. "C'mon," he said, "don't be bashful."

The sun rose low and so piercingly bright we had to turn our backs to it. But the brilliant light held no warmth. Slowly, as slowly as possible, we peeled off parkas, flannel shirts, mukluks and pants, right down to our long underwear tops and bottoms. "Hats too," said Jerry, pointing at the knit stocking caps both of us wore beneath our parka hoods. "And gloves. You can leave your socks on. We've got time."

How much time? I wondered. On a normal day, Andy would already be at my house, sipping his coffee, laughing about something he'd heard on the Tundra

Times radio show: 'To Jimmy Charlie out in Huslia, your wife Sylvia had a nine-pound-ten-ounce baby girl. Sylvia and the baby will be flying home on Tuesday.'

"That baby's as big as he is," Andy would laugh while talking about going back to Italy, and complaining about the coffee from the red can that, according to him, *never* means good taste.

Of course, there were some mornings he didn't come. What if this was one of them? Would he get here before we were unconscious? Would he be able to do anything to help us if he did? As if in answer to my question, came a rifle shot from the far shore. It echoed and re-echoed in the cold, clear air, sounding like many shots, as if many people had come to rescue us. But it was just one shot. It was Andy.

Shivering, fingers in armpits, I looked at Evie who looked at me. Jerry drove the bolt on the sniper rifle, then looked around at the two of us. "You don't look too confident," he said. "How come you're not prayin' or something?" He checked the riverbank a full quarter mile away, fiddled with an adjustment on the scope, then looked back. "Go ahead," he said, "huddle up. Won't save you though. And I want you both to come stand here, kind of in front of me. That's the way. I like this," he said. "See how the 'great sniper' has to come out here with his ordinary rifle and make a really tough shot into the sun."

I took Evie in my arms, holding her with my hands in fists to try to protect my fingers, and turning her out of the breeze. It had only been minutes since we'd undressed, but already there was very little heat to share and we both were shivering hard. One blessing: I knew this wouldn't take long.

"I'm glad I got to know you," she said, "before …"

"Me too."

"Our father," she began, and I joined in.

"Rudy said that, too," said Jerry. "Didn't help him either."

Over on the riverbank I saw Andy step into view. Jerry raised the rifle, sighted, drew his breath and fired. Andy waved a moosehide mitt at him. "Shit!" said Jerry, and ejected the spent cartridge. "Slow down," I heard him tell himself. "You can get this guy."

"Thy kingdom come," we continued, shivering violently.

As Andy dropped his wave, he shook his mitt free and in a smooth movement levered a shell into the chamber as he raised a rifle that looked a lot like my father's carbine. I remembered the last time I'd seen him make that move with that rifle, how the caribou dropped to the river ice and how we cheered.

"Hah," crowed Jerry. He had turned toward us, happy—triumphant even—and his Tanana Valley Fair marksman emblem, dangling from his zipper pull, flashed fire in the sun. As Jerry turned back, we heard a zipping sound. A perfectly round hole about the diameter of my little finger appeared in the marksman medal. Jerry's body jerked and the rifle fell from his grip. As he looked down at his ruined medal, incredulous, the report from the carbine finally overtook us.

"Cheez," gasped Jerry. "Good shot!" He coughed a spatter of blood into his glove and his knees buckled, dropping him to the ice. He drew a ragged breath, coughed again and looked up at me, his chin blood-washed, trying to pull off his goofy grin. "Bless me Father," he said, sagging forward, "for I have …"

"Sinned." I said.

He fell on his face, his body gold-washed by the early sun, never moving again. Looking up from shivered last rites, I saw Andy half-jogging toward us, his right arm cradled and bloody. I knew it wasn't over yet. Evie and I were very cold, Andy was injured and we were a long way from town. So I turned from the business of the dying back to the business of living.

CHAPTER 35

"Can I show you my breasts?" Evie asked. She had come into my office late morning on a Tuesday in February, this time closing both sets of curtains then coming around my desk to stand beside me.

I must have grinned. "This happens to me all the time," I said. That's when she began to blush. I swiveled my chair to face her and she unbuttoned a white blouse and raised a lacy bra to display what appeared to be an identical set of healthy breasts. I looked at them carefully.

"Touch," she said. I stood up and directed her to my chair. As before, she sat and drew my hand to cup her left breast. Again, her lower breast was cool against my fingers. The top of the breast, under my thumb at about eleven o'clock, that had been raised and red and sore looking, was also smooth and cool to the touch. I smiled at her as she stood and put herself back together.

"It's gone," she said.

"Remission," I said. "But if it was cancer, it could come back."

"I know," she said, "but I'll take this for now." Her eyes met mine. "I know you had something to do with this. Don't think I haven't heard about your 'prayer squad.'"

Now I blushed. "There really aren't any secrets here, are there?"

"Maybe one," she said.

News of Jerry's death had seemed to spread almost cabin to cabin on the wind. Andy was a local hero for his dramatic rescue of Evie and me, and so far Jerry's part in it had been put off to what locals generally considered 'cabin fever'—too much time alone and too much alcohol. The one genuine local secret, at least so far, was our own international spy ring: Masterson's stealing and trying to sell radar secrets, Frankie's plan to transmit those secrets to the enemy, and the active local presence of East German spies to bring in the cash and help make sure it all happened.

Part and parcel of it all was the role William played, including saving our lives. Ribs knit, he was now back at work at the school, sweeping, mopping and washing blackboards. He said his handlers back in the motherland thought he'd been injured a lot more grievously than he had been, and agreed that this recovery period would be a good time for him to pursue the U.S. citizenship that had become his dream, his reasons quite different from theirs.

Standing out on the river ice at nearly forty below, in our long underwear, deeply chilled with Jerry down and dead and Andy bleeding, it had all seemed very close to the edge. All the what-ifs: if Andy hadn't come for his coffee that morning, if Jerry hadn't rushed his shot, if Evie and I had been out there another ten or twenty minutes, to lapse into unconsciousness as our core body temperatures dropped—or to get so cold that, even if help did come—the shock of rewarming stopped our hearts, as often happened. And then, the biggest what-if of all: if Andy had walked out from town, slowly tracking us, instead of—as he did—grabbing my truck keys and rifle, driving out quickly, heater on full bore.

We were painwracked and stumbling with cold-contracted muscles; dazed, muttering and nearly incoherent with advancing hypothermia, but Andy somehow managed to shepherd both of us back into most of our clothing and across the long ice to the wind shadow of the Mission and the blessing of that truck, so close and so quickly warm.

Jerry's shot at Andy had drifted wide. It was not the trophy heart shot he desired, but a furrow plowed through flesh and muscle of both the side of Andy's chest and his upper bicep—two flesh wounds—with the bullet passing under his armpit and away. Doubtless painful and ugly looking, he was back chopping his own wood before the gossip faded.

"I need to tell you I'm leaving," said Evie. I smiled, but the news was like one of those sharp punches to the chest you don't see coming, that both knocks the last breath out of you while making it difficult and painful to draw the next.

I heard my front door open and Andy's voice. "Is there coffee?" Evie's eyes met mine.

"I have to tell him, too," she said. We rose and met Andy hanging up his parka and mitts, and moved in a line down the short hallway to the kitchen. "I'll make coffee," said Evie lightly. "You boys sit." So we sat, watching Evie make coffee, which had acquired a sudden poignancy, now that I knew this tumultuous part of both of our lives was winding down.

When she came to the table she sat next to me instead of sitting next to Andy as she typically had. Andy and I both noticed, and he raised his eyebrows at me.

"I need to tell both of you," she began.

"Wait," said Andy, "I have something I need to tell both of you."

Evie and I were so caught up in her news, we must have gaped at him. "I'm going away," he said, "going back to Italy, back to the Mediterranean." He pulled a long envelope from the pocket of his plaid flannel shirt. "Here's my ticket, Pan American out of Fairbanks. I fly to Anchorage, Annette Island, Seattle, Chicago, New York, London and Rome." He looked up at us, beaming. "And I leave next Tuesday."

"But how," asked Evie.

"Totally anonymous," he said. "The ticket came in the mail with my name on it." His eyes met mine. "This is a dream come true," he said, "and I want to thank you."

"Thank Frankie," I said. By then we had our coffee so I proposed a toast: "To Frankie, wherever he may be."

"I think we know where he is," muttered Andy, but he raised his mug and sipped Frankie's good health. "God, that's awful coffee," he said, "but that's the way I like it."

We were laughing. We often laughed together, the three of us, and I knew that was the way I'd remember us. Andy looked at Evie. "He's not sending you away, too?"

"No, my idea, but I'm going less far," she said, looking at her hands and at her steaming mug. "I'm going to school. I'm going to apply to the University of Washington in Seattle, so I don't have to go too far from home, and I'm hoping to be, maybe a teacher. I'm really not sure. To tell you the God's honest truth, which is one of the new skills I'm developing, I've spent so much time preparing to die, that preparing to

231

live sort of has me buffaloed. It's funny how it happened. The other night, before I went to bed, I knelt down to try praying. I figured I'd start easy. I said 'Now I lay me down to sleep' but then I didn't get any further. Right in the middle of my prayer I thought, *I'll go to college*."

Andy grinned at her. "Sounds to me like you're already getting results." He shook his head. "I'm really proud of you and really happy."

Later, after Evie had gone, Andy looked at me more seriously. "I need to level with you," he said.

"No you don't."

"I feel like I do. I haven't been completely up front with you, and now," he nodded at the ticket in his pocket, "especially with this, I need to be honest."

"Is this about being homosexual?" Andy's mouth fell open.

"Gay," he said.

"What's 'gay'?" I asked.

"It's what we homos call ourselves because it sounds so much better than homo. But," he hesitated, "how did you know? Did Evie tell you?"

I said, "I think you know enough about Evie to know she wouldn't give up any of your secrets."

"Yeah," he said, "I know that, too. But how did you know?"

"People talked around it," I said. "Jerry said something like 'just because you don't look at pictures of naked women.' And out at the burning boat, when William was explaining about spies who are moles, he said something about someone who is 'with you but not of you, not unlike yourself.' And he was talking to you. Somehow he had found out, which I guess isn't that surprising for a spy."

"You don't seem too upset," said Andy. "The Bible says …"

"I know," I said. "And I can't explain it. My thought is that after all is said and done, the Bible was translated by men and may not be entirely as originally intended. I believe we're all created by God and I'm not qualified to turn thumbs down on any of the works of the Lord. And after all you and I have been through these past months, I just feel lucky to have you for my friend."

He shook my hand, smiled and let out a long breath. I could see he was relieved and I felt bad that he had to be. We stood a long moment. "I've got to go pack," he said.

"You don't leave for a week, and you don't have that much stuff."

"I know," he said. "I'll probably do it a couple of times, just for the fun."

~

If Francine was surprised to see the marshal, she didn't let on. She was dressed mostly in black, as if mourning. I couldn't help remembering that the last time I'd seen her she'd been mostly naked. Clothed or not, she'd be hard to forget.

She nodded at the introduction, extended a slim hand to the marshal and settled demurely into my guest chair.

"Did you mean to kill Frankie?" I asked her.

She blinked at me, surprised and licked her lips. "Not at first," she said. "I just thought I could talk him into giving Jerry the money he owed him."

"So you and Jerry could leave Alaska, go back to Sausalito and settle in."

233

A tear escaped the side of one eye and streaked her cheek. "Frankie owed it to him," she said. "He was holding out. It was making Jerry depressed and sad. I thought I could help."

"It wasn't hard to get Frankie out to somewhere private, was it?" She shook her head. "You undressed?" She nodded.

"I don't want you to think …" she began. "I just knew it was the quickest way to get him to go—the easiest way."

"Why did he think you were going all the way out there?"

"Well, I told him I wanted to talk to him, privately, where no one could possibly intrude. But I know he hoped … umm," she said. "First he took me to his place. He showed me everything, his darkroom, his library of classics—though I don't even think he could read—even showed me his pornography. When he showed me the Bible with the two little pistols in it, I took one when he wasn't looking, just in case."

"What went wrong?" I asked.

"First, he lied to me," she said. "We went all the way out there to that old boat in a big Sno-Cat, and when we got there, he said he wasn't going to give Jerry any of the money. Any. It wasn't fair! I had already told Mum and Daddy we'd be moving down there soon, buying a house. They even found a house they thought we might like. Pink, near the beach. I guess I still thought I might be able to change his mind so I let him undress me, and … but then after, when we were walking down a little trail, he started laughing at me, and said 'just wait 'til I tell Jerry.' And I knew there wasn't going to be a house for us in Sausalito."

234

"What happened next," I asked. "Did he grab you or try to hurt you?" She smiled at me, and over her shoulder I saw the marshal lean forward in his chair, listening intently, with a pad on his knee and pencil scribbling furiously.

"You're very kind," she said. "But no, he didn't grab me. I went to him with my arms open, and when he pulled me close—and told me Jerry would never leave Alaska with me—I pulled the little pistol out of my pocket and put it up under his chin. 'You won't,' he said, but I did. Here it is." She pulled the missing ivory-handled Derringer out of her pocket, by the barrel, and set it gently on my desk.

"You did one more thing," I said.

"I spread his arms and legs apart. So he looked like an X there in the snow. I thought an airplane might see him and land. I had heard about wolves finding bodies and didn't want that to happen to him, even if he was a liar." She shivered. "I know Jerry had his faults," she said, "but he really loved me. We would have been happy."

After the marshal put her in the airplane, he stepped down again to shake my hand. "What will happen?" I asked.

"Missing some of the cards in her deck, I think. Might get off," he said, as usual, carefully conserving his words.

It was just about two thirty and still daylight when the plane lifted off the river ice and circled toward Fairbanks. The temperature was in the low minus twenties for a change, nearly balmy, and I could sense the extra sunlight and the days beginning to get longer. So much had happened here. Frankie was dead, Jerry was dead, the East Germans were dead—no one

235

knew what had happened to Masterson—though I had my suspicions. In a few days Andy would fly back to his beloved Italy for strong doses of real Italian coffee—that didn't come out of a can of *any* color—and a chance to find a life less lonely.

For a while it seemed like I might have found someone like that right here in Chandelar, but now she would be leaving too, which was okay. In my heart of hearts I was still in love with someone who still literally haunted my dreams. Which was also okay.

I drove Andy to Fairbanks, to the airport, in the church's new pickup truck. He was ready to take the train. "You saved my life," I told him. "The least I can do is help you leave."

"Thanks," he said. "I think."

I walked him out to the plane, a huge, propeller-driven Lockheed Super Constellation in Pan Am blue. On the far wing, a propeller began to spin slowly, fired with a puff of blue smoke, then throttled up to a steady roar as the next propeller began to turn.

Andy hesitated on the bottom step, turned and shook my hand again. "Safe travels," I said. "God speed," raising my voice to be heard over the racket.

As we stood looking at each other, the weeks and months of life in Chandelar played back through my head like one of Friday night's newsreels at the Pioneers of Alaska Hall. Andy, my first friend in Chandelar, had been so much a part of it all.

"Gonna miss you," I said.

He laughed. "You know I won't always be in Italy. I'll be back. Probably sooner than you think."

"In that case," I said, "bring back some decent coffee."

Made in United States
Troutdale, OR
08/17/2023